THE HOUSE
ON THE MOON

The House
on the Moon

by

Georgina Bruce

BLACK SHUCK
SHADOWS

Black Shuck Books
www.BlackShuckBooks.co.uk

Cover design & internal layout © WHITEspace 2023
www.white-space.uk

First published in the UK by Black Shuck Books, 2023

978-1-913038-93-9

Don't Be Clever

It was impossible to see the house on the moon with the naked eye, but Dee insisted that she could.

"Well, it's more like *sense*, rather than see," she said. "I'm a HSP. You know what that is? A Highly Sensitive Person."

"That's nice," said Suzanne, looking out of the window. She'd given up trying to read her book, Brian Cox's recent *Moon House Mystery*. Every time she picked it up, the loud Californian woman gently put her hand over Suzanne's and pushed it down again.

"How can you read?" she said. "You'll get motion sickness. You want some Dramamine?"

They were on a bus, travelling on a fast, narrow road, surrounded by granite mountains. Every so often, a turquoise sea slipped out from between buildings and trees, startling Suzanne with a flash of beauty. She felt very far away from home, and wasn't sure if that was a good thing.

"It's difficult being a HSP," said Dee. "To feel so much more deeply than normal people do. The house appearing really messed up my chakras. I'm just raw right now, spiritually speaking."

"Hmm." Suzanne glanced at her watch. Another fifteen minutes and they'd be at the bus station in Split. Soon she'd be on a high-speed catamaran, heading for a blue-green island overflowing with vineyards and encircled by wild beaches. Alone. It was a strange thought. A guilty thought, even. To assuage her conscience, she decided to be nice to the crazy woman sitting beside her. She could tolerate her for fifteen minutes, couldn't she? After all, it's nice to be nice.

"Do you think there are people in the house on the moon?" Suzanne asked. It seemed to her that there must be. What was the point of a house without people?

"No, I'd sense them if there were. Like I sensed the house. My energies were all over the place. Like my tidal energies? You know we have tides? We're mostly water."

You're mostly water, thought Suzanne. Then again, she'd been feeling out of sorts for a while, too. Even before the news about the house on the moon came out, she'd been in a funk. She felt weird; she didn't know how to explain it. She'd been less patient with Joe, for a start. He'd really got on her last nerve, to be honest. And when the kids had rung from their university halls, asking for money, she couldn't be bothered with them, either. She'd handed the phone over to Joe and gone upstairs to run a bath. Maybe it was the time of life. The change. That's what she'd been thinking. But then the news came out about the house on the moon, and she'd thought, well, there you go. Not saying that explained anything – really it was a total mystery, even Brian Cox thought so – but it certainly put things into perspective. If *that* can happen, she'd thought, anything can happen. All the rules can be thrown out the window.

She'd booked this holiday on the joint credit card, telling Joe he should be grateful it was only for two weeks, that she was actually planning on coming back.

"Alright," he said. "If you want to do your Shirley Valentine impression, I suppose I can't stop you."

"Shirley Valentine? Hey Joe, the eighties called. They want their pop culture reference back."

"Don't be clever, Suzanne," he said.

Don't be clever. Well, didn't that just take the biscuit. She wondered if anyone had ever told Dee not to be clever, and doubted it, and then admonished herself for being so mean.

"I'm an empath," Dee was saying, "so I can tell that you're a good and kind person. You don't have to tell me, of course, but I'm wondering what you're going through right now that means you need to be away from your family."

Suzanne glared at the woman, annoyed at her for peering into her thoughts. Maybe she really *was* an empath. But no: Suzanne remembered she was wearing her wedding ring. And she'd been scrolling through family pictures before Dee plonked herself down on the seat beside her. It was sly, though. Suzanne didn't like that, even though she agreed she was a good and kind person, actually. But then, wasn't everyone? Deep down.

"I don't need to be away from them," said Suzanne. "I just fancied a holiday."

"Me too!" Dee exclaimed. "We are kindred spirits, Suzie! I just knew we would be. It was fate that I sat next to you on this bus. I tell you, my husband thinks I'm a kook. Well, what he doesn't know is that I'm divorcing him the second I get back to California. That guy. All he does is watch TV. Can you believe it?"

Isn't that all anyone does, Suzanne wondered. It was all she and Joe did. Get up, go to work, come home, have tea in front of the telly, go to bed. What else were they supposed to do? Explore each other's chakras? But again, Dee was right in another way. Ever since she'd found out about the house on the moon, Suzanne had been wondering if there wasn't something more to life. How did people live in the house on the moon? They weren't watching Netflix every night, Suzanne was sure of that.

"Well you and me, Suzie, we are going to set some fires! We're going to show these men!"

Suzanne smiled politely, and turned back to the window. There was a good view of the sea now, and then the bus turned into another busy road, where there was a big, ancient-looking wall and hundreds of people in shorts and bikinis, eating gelato.

"I guess we're here," she said.

"I'm going to tell him: Jack, it's over. You can keep the house. I'm going to move into the condo. There's a yoga studio in the building and my yoga teacher, well... he gets me, you know? On a soul level. Oh my gosh, look at that sea! Isn't it just perfect? I can't wait to baptise myself in it. You know what I do? Wherever I go, I pick up a stone and take it home with me. Did you ever hear of something like that before? My husband thinks I'm a kook!"

Suzanne shook her head, picturing the windowsill of their bathroom at home, lined with shells and stones from various beach trips and holidays.

"I get a feeling," said Dee, "and I pick a stone up and it's like, the right stone for me. It sounds crazy, I know. But you see, I'm a shaman. You know what a shaman is?"

"Yes," said Suzanne.

"Well a shaman is someone who can communicate between our world and the spirit world. So when I pick up these stones, it's like I'm getting a message from the spirit world. It's coming through me. It's quite a responsibility."

"I can imagine."

The bus was slowing down now, pulling across the road. A cacophony of cars, screeching and honking, broke out around them, followed by the deep mournful sound of a boat's horn echoing through the air. Suzanne saw the ferry port on her right, and then the bus was stopping.

Dee was apparently waiting for everyone else to get off the bus before she stood up, so Suzanne said, "Sorry, I just need to... I have to get to my ferry."

"Oh, sure! Let's go," said Dee.

Out of the vehicle, the hot air swamped Suzanne. This was a mistake, she thought. She'd never liked the heat, or crowds, and hadn't she been seasick that time she and Joe took the ferry to France? But it was too late now. She lost the annoying Californian in the crowd of people grabbing their suitcases, and made her way across the street to the port.

~

Her boat was called *Puntamika*. It was as crowded as the bus had been, but she managed to get a seat next to a smeared, dirty window, and as the ferry slowly chugged away from the harbour, she felt relief. The captain made an announcement about journey times being unaffected by the house on the moon, and the passengers all grinned at each other, as if the house was funny. Which in a way, Suzanne thought, it was. Funny how there could suddenly be a house on the moon, and yet life went on down here completely normally. The town of

Split grew distant, and acres of blue sea spread out around her, sparkling in the sunshine. For the first time in nearly twenty-four hours, ever since the fight with Joe and the early morning taxi to Manchester airport, Suzanne felt her eyelids drooping down, and she gratefully slipped into a dreamless sleep.

She had no idea how long she'd been sleeping when she felt a jostling at her elbow, and a now-familiar voice saying, "Oh would you mind? So kind! It's just we're friends, you see."

Suzanne cracked one eye open to observe the quiet man beside her getting up and wiry, loud Dee wriggling into his place.

"Oh my gosh!" Dee grabbed her wrist and squeezed it, a little too hard. Her long nails dug into Suzanne's skin. "I thought I'd lost you at the bus station! Didn't you hear me calling you?"

Suzanne shook her head. It was a lie. She had heard Dee calling her, but she'd walked away quickly, pretending to be rushing for her ferry.

"Well here you are! It's fate! This morning when I woke up, I had a feeling that something good would happen. I didn't know what it would be, but then I met you! Isn't that wild?"

"Wild," said Suzanne, rubbing her eyes and struggling to sit upright in her seat.

A voice came through the loudspeakers. "Dear passengers," it said. "The next stop is Korčula. Korčula, next stop."

Oh thank God, thought Suzanne. I'm here at last.

"Did he say Korchla? I'm going to Korkooler. You think that's what he meant?"

Suzanne frowned. "It doesn't sound like the same place," she said, hopefully.

"Wait, I'm going to ask someone," said Dee.

She got up from her seat and made her way back towards the bathroom area. When Dee was out of sight, Suzanne retrieved her suitcase from the pile at the front of the boat, and made her way to the exit. She was halfway along the jetty when Dee trotted up breathlessly beside her.

"It's the same damn place!" she said. "He was just saying it wrong. I guess that's how they say it here. But they should say it in a way people can understand."

Suzanne nodded. Was she ever going to get rid of this annoying woman?

"You're so kind, Suzie," she was saying. "I knew from the moment I saw you. I said to myself, here is a deeply kind, wise, and spiritual woman. I just know these things! Don't ask me how!"

I won't, Suzanne muttered to herself.

She took her mobile phone from her pocket and waited for it to re-set itself to EU roaming. No missed calls. Not that she was expecting any. There was a line of taxis in the ferry car park, so she turned to Dee and said, "It was so nice meeting you. Well, I'm going to jump in a taxi. Have a great holiday."

"Wait," said Dee. "We need to swap numbers. Where are you staying? Nearby?"

"Lumbarda," said Suzanne. "It's quite a way from here. So I guess this is goodbye."

"No freaking way! Lumbarda? That's where I'm headed! This is just so unbelievable, right? This is fate! You know I was telling myself how great it was to be alone but then when I met you I thought wouldn't it be even more great to have a friend to do things with? Who wants to vacation by themselves, right? Hey, let's get this cab. We can share."

Suzanne watched Dee stride over to the taxi driver, making no attempt to speak his language, but trying to haggle his price down to pennies.

"It's okay," said Suzanne to the driver, "I'll pay. It's fine."

She smiled at him, trying to convey her sympathy and her own embarrassment, plus the fact that she really wasn't associated with this woman in any way and wouldn't choose to be sharing a taxi with her, only she couldn't really say no now on account of how she'd made the mistake of letting her know where she was going. It was a bit much for a smile to convey, and the taxi driver just shook his head, and shoved their cases in the boot.

"You have to haggle," Dee said. "You can't be such a pushover! Stand up for yourself, girl."

"It's fine," said Suzanne. "I don't think this is a haggling kind of place."

"Well I don't know. I don't want to get ripped off."

"We're not getting ripped off." *I'm* getting ripped off, thought Suzanne. By *you*.

The taxi took them out of town, along narrow roads that wound through vineyards, past a quarry and a cemetery, and then the view opened up onto a huge bay that curved around into mountains.

"Wow," said Suzanne. "It's breathtaking."

"It's fate," said Dee. "We were meant to be here, in this time and place. It's the universe aligning."

Suzanne thanked the universe that it hadn't aligned them into the same hotel. She got out of the taxi, paid the driver, bid goodbye to Dee, and pretended not to hear her pleas to meet up for dinner. The taxi driver had finally got the hang of the situation, and drove off while Dee was still reciting her phone number out of the window. At last, the car disappeared out of sight.

Suzanne stood facing the sea, then she crossed the road to the tiny strip of sandy beach, took off her trainers and socks and stepped into the water. It was crystal clear, beautiful, and felt as refreshing as a new day.

~

Her hotel room had a little balcony, and Suzanne sat there to watch the sun go down and eat a slice of pizza she'd bought from the restaurant downstairs. Perfect. She thought back over the previous day. Had she done everything she needed to do? Was everything in its place? She thought so. Joe's clothes in a pile on the stairs, ready to go up. His tea in the oven, ready to be heated through. Meals in the freezer, enough to last him for a couple of weeks. The timings were the only thing she worried about. The two weeks she had here ought to give her the space she needed – but life was unpredictable.

As the moon rose over the dark waters, she squinted upwards, trying to make out the house that was perched there, like a little hat. You could see it with a telescope, of course, but you couldn't get a telescope for love or money these days. Amazon sold out the day after the news broke. Joe thought he had an old telescope in the garage, but there was a lot of junk in there he'd never bothered clearing out, and in the end he decided it was too much trouble to go looking. And Suzanne thought it was nonsense anyway. Why would Joe have a telescope? Since when was he interested in the stars? Since when was he interested in anything other than the football and sinking a few pints at the weekend? But why was that bothering her now? She'd been happy enough. She'd never minded him until recently; at least, she couldn't remember minding. It was the house that had changed everything. It made it seem like life had more possibilities. Like that life was a hell of a lot more interesting than she'd been giving it credit for.

"It's the menopause, love," Joe had said. "I heard about it in Sainsbury's. You're the right age for it and everything. It said you'd have mood swings and be irritable."

"I'm not fucking irritable," Suzanne said.

Joe raised his eyebrows.

"I swear to God, Joe."

But Joe hadn't listened. That was the thing, Suzanne thought. He never really listened.

Were the people on the moon listening? She thought they must be. Despite whatever Brian Cox might say in his bestselling book, Suzanne thought there was only one good explanation for the house on the moon. The Earth had neighbours – and they were twitching their curtains. Suzanne bet they had a telescope, too.

She wondered if she could rent a telescope from one of the rental places in Lumbarda. She'd seen mopeds and bicycles and those little electric scooters; maybe they'd have telescopes too. Anything tourists wanted, they had. Maybe she'd hire a moped and explore the island. She imagined what Joe would have to say about that: he'd roll his eyes and make a joke about her falling off. She'd fallen off her bike *once*, years ago when they first got together. She'd given birth to two children since then. Driven up and down the country to care for her parents when they got sick. Been promoted to Head of Department at school. But to Joe, she'd always be Clumsy Sue. Don't try to be clever, Clumsy Sue.

Well, not anymore. That wasn't her anymore.

She went over her plan again as she went to bed. Her own bed, all to herself. She wouldn't have to make this bed. She wouldn't have to strip the bed or wash the sheets or wrestle with the duvet. She didn't even have to make her own breakfast. These thoughts were relaxing, and she soon drifted off to sleep.

~

It was days before she ran into Dee again. She'd caught glimpses of her hanging around the hotel, and she always made sure to check out of the window before stepping outside. She'd heard her, too, her voice echoing above the gentle crash of waves and the scrape of chairs against paved floors in cafes. She knew, of course, that she wouldn't be able to avoid Dee forever – Lumbarda was a small place, and it was coming to the end of the season, so it was getting harder to lose herself in a crowd. In some ways, it would be easier to get it over with – rip off the plaster – but she just didn't want to. All she wanted to do was sleep, eat, go to one of the beaches in the afternoon and swim in the calm, clear water. People left her alone here. No one got on her nerves the way they did at home. Waiters ignored her, smiled wryly at her stumbling attempts to speak the language, but otherwise didn't bother her. No one interrupted her halfway through a meal to check that everything was okay for her. Everything was okay. It was better than okay. She should have done this years ago, she thought. She remembered all those holidays with Joe and the kids, trying to wash their clothes in a campsite bathroom, or washing up tiny plates and cups in a tiny sink, while rain battered the plastic windows of the caravan. Then, when the kids were older and she and Joe had more money, going to all-inclusive resorts, watching Joe knock back free Piña Coladas, dreading having to sleep next to his snoring, farting, holiday body. Was that fair? Hadn't she had fun? She must have done. She wouldn't have put up with it otherwise. But this – this was something else. It was beautiful, breathtaking. Miraculous. Lying on a beach in the sunshine with nothing to do and no one to bother her – heaven. She thought she might even manage to make a start on her book this afternoon. Maybe Brian Cox could explain her to herself.

But there was Dee. She was trotting towards her from the other end of the beach, her tanned and wiry arms and legs exposed by her yellow swimsuit. Dyed-blonde hair under her straw hat that she pressed to her head with one hand, while the other hand waved up and down like she was flagging a taxi.

"Suzie! Suzie, oh my gosh!"

Suzanne sighed and stretched out her legs. There were still droplets of sea water on her knees. She looked at them sparkling in the sunshine. Everything evaporates, she thought. Even beautiful things must come to an end.

"Hi Dee," she said. "How are you?"

"Thank God I found you," said Dee. She sat down on Suzanne's towel. "I was looking for you all over. I came to your hotel! They didn't tell you?"

Suzanne shook her head. She'd told the receptionists to say that she wasn't staying there, but she wasn't sure how much they'd understood. And now she felt a little bad about that. Would it really hurt her to spend a couple of hours with this woman? Okay, she was crazy and annoying, but she was a sister of sorts. A woman on her own. Suzanne could afford to be a little generous. And maybe Dee could be useful to her. In fact, that should have occurred to her before now – that she might need a friend, later.

"Gosh, they never told me," she said. "Never mind. You're here now."

"I sure am! And don't you think it's fate, how we keep getting brought together? There's something about you Suzie, I don't know what it is. But something makes me feel we're connected. Do you feel it?"

Suzanne shook her head. "Not really."

"Well listen, I'm a HSP and an empath. And I'm telling you, something—" (and here she jabbed Suzanne's knee with a pointy finger) "—something has brought us together."

"Okay," said Suzanne.

"And it has to do with the house on the moon. So tell me, tell me about the first time you saw it. I was with my yoga teacher, he was showing me the constellations."

"Oh yeah? Is that a yoga position, or a euphemism?"

"Don't be a smartass, Suzie," Dee snapped.

Suzanne flinched. But then Dee's face relaxed and she smiled.

"Alright, I admit it," she said. "He's younger than me. But he's very wise. Some people just have old souls, don't they? He doesn't have any money, that's his problem. But I can help with that. Listen, when I divorce my husband, I'm going to be so rich. He has no idea what's coming. You ever been divorced?"

"No. I've only ever been married to Joe."

"Joe? That's your husband? So why isn't he here? I can tell you why my lump of a so-called husband isn't here. Can't tear himself away from the television, that's why. He thinks I'm kooky, wanting to go on vacation. Why can't we go to Florida, he says, like we always do? Florida! Have you ever been there? My god, Suzie, it's the worst. Never go to Florida, okay? I'm telling you. You'll get eaten by a god-damn crocodile. But listen, tell me about your husband. Why'd you leave him at home?"

"He's great," Suzanne said. "He's a really good guy. Really." She stood up. "I'm going for a swim," she said.

"Oh yay! I'm a water baby, too. I just love it. You know what, I'm going to come in with you. Okay! Just wait for me to get my things, I've left them all the way over there. Hang on... Oh okay, I'll see you in the water! See you there!"

The sea was shallow until a long way out, but Suzanne kept wading. She supposed Dee would be a strong swimmer, what with living by the beach in California. Whereas she, Suzanne, was not confident in the water at all. She was scared of riptides, sea urchins, choking. She weighed up her options. *Don't be a smartass*, she thought. When the sea reached her hips, she dived forward and began a weak breaststroke, feeling buoyed up by the salty water. It was glorious, actually.

"The moon affects the oceans, doesn't it?" Dee was beside her already, chatting away in her ear. "But the water feels the same to me. What about you? I know you're not a shaman or anything, but I'm wondering if you'd noticed anything. You're a very observant person."

"You don't know anything about me," said Suzanne.

Dee laughed. "I know, but I feel I do! I feel like this was meant to be."

~

When Suzanne finally managed to get away from Dee that afternoon, retreating to her hotel under the pretext of a headache, she felt more anxious than she had at any point in this whole experience. She checked her phone again. Nothing. Then she unpacked her laptop and went online, looking at her facebook page in case anyone was trying to get in touch with her. She scrolled the local news, then the Manchester news, then the nationals. There were still a lot of stories about the house. A lot of theories. People thought it was either something to do with Elon Musk, or aliens. Astronomers and astrologers were interviewed on the BBC news. She watched a YouTube video in which Jordan Peterson talked about the destabilising effect of anomalous objects on human psychology, but after a few minutes she got bored and clicked on a Baker Fleet video. Her most famous hit: *Heart like a knife*. It was Suzanne's favourite song, but just now she found it insipid. She shut the laptop.

Suzanne hadn't liked Dee's questions, her interrogation on the beach. Of course she loved her husband. Of course she did. It wasn't about love, or the lack of it. She just needed some space. But the questions made her nervous. Okay, Suzanne reassured herself. Everything's fine. We had that argument before I left, that's why he hasn't called. Should I call him? Call the house? Yes, I should do that. Do both things.

Joe's mobile went straight to answerphone. "Hi love," Suzanne said. "Missing you. Call me when you get this." Then she rang the landline, listened to the phone ringing out. She pictured Joe's clothes, all in a neat pile on the stair. He always stepped over things on the stairs, rather than carry them up. The thought made her feel sad, rather than infuriated. She decided to call him again tomorrow.

That night, she was restless. The bed that had been so comfortable now felt too big for her. The curtains didn't fully close and she was aware, all night, of the big moon beaming above her, the moon with its incongruous house, that alien object influencing her psychology. Maybe. Or maybe she was asleep and dreaming. She really couldn't tell.

~

She got up early the next morning and headed to the little jetty off Lumbarda beach, to get the sea taxi to Badija Island. She had a big bag which held her swimming costume, towel, snorkel, bottle of water, sandwich, half a bottle of wine and the Brian Cox book that she still hadn't managed to crack open. Bliss. She'd heard the island was uninhabited except for the monks in the fourteenth-century monastery, and some friendly deer. The hotel receptionist assured her she'd be able to find a little private cove where she could sunbathe and swim to her heart's content. It was going to be a perfect day.

The water taxi was waiting at the jetty and she climbed aboard. It was a beautiful day, and she said so to the captain, in her best Croatian. "Predivan dan danas," she said, and he grinned. "One minute we go, lady," he said, clearly not fooled by her best attempt at the accent. He unhooked the rope from the jetty, and climbed around the boat, making his preparations, then sat at the front and started the engines. He was good looking, Suzanne thought. She'd noticed that Croatian men were generally quite tall. She liked that. Maybe she'd think about that later, in her private cove on the almost-uninhabited island.

But just as they were drifting out of the dock, the captain stopped and reversed them back in again. "One more passenger comes," he said.

She was trotting along the jetty, one hand holding on to her straw hat.

"Fuck my life," said Suzanne.

"Oh my gosh!" Dee said, clambering into the boat.

"I know," said Suzanne. "It's fate."

"It's fate! It must be. You know what, it's the moon. It was a full moon last night. I felt it in my whole body."

The boat's engine as they cut through the water was too loud for conversation, not that it stopped Dee from trying. Suzanne kept up her own inner monologue, bewailing her so-called fate. How was it, in this most beautiful place, a place where it should have been easy to be alone – which was all she wanted, by the way – that she was besieged, yes, besieged, no actually, harassed – harassed by this woman with her stupid voice and her stupid ideas? Was this really her fate? Why? What had she ever done to deserve this? Then she thought, maybe she did deserve it, actually. Maybe she was just getting what was coming to her. And look, she told herself, there's nothing wrong with her except she's just a bit irritating. That's all. My god, Suzanne, she berated herself. Have some patience! Be kind!

At Badija, they disembarked. The fragile hope Suzanne had carried that Dee might be going to a different island vaporised into the clear, fragrant air. There was nothing she could do. She was stuck, and she had to make the best of it. Be kind, she reminded herself. The same injunctions she'd been hearing all her life. Don't be clever, Suzanne. Be nice.

They walked along the stony path with the sea to their left and the forest to their right. It was breathtakingly lovely, like nowhere Suzanne had ever been. Dee kept up a monologue about how similar it was to California, except for the kinds of trees, which were maybe a bit different, but then it was more about the feeling of the trees, their spirits, because all things have a spirit, don't they, she said. And she, being a shaman, and a Highly Sensitive Person, was able to connect to those spirits in a way a normal person couldn't.

"The spirits here are very strong," she said. "Very powerful. I'm not sure they're altogether positive, though. They feel like maybe they don't want us here. I wouldn't want to be here alone!"

I would, Suzanne said, under her breath. She hadn't noticed anything weird about the trees. Then again, it wasn't easy to commune with the spirits of the island while Dee was wittering on at her.

There were many little coves and beaches along their way. Suzanne nurtured a tiny dream that she could still get one of these places all to herself.

"Wouldn't you love to be alone, swimming there, by yourself, with no one else in the world?" she said, pointing to an idyllic-looking bay below the path.

"Well sure!" Dee said. "If I didn't have you!"

Fine. Have it your way, thought Suzanne.

They walked around to the far side of the island, and Suzanne pointed out a little bay tucked away below some rocks. They had to climb down from the path, and when they got there, Suzanne realised the trees above had been hiding another patch of beach a little way behind them. Perfect.

"Let's head there," she said.

"This is beautiful," said Dee.

It was the first honest, simple thing Suzanne had heard her say, and she rewarded her with a smile. Probably shouldn't encourage her, thought Suzanne, but she couldn't exactly take it back. Be kind!

They took out their towels and spread them over the rocks. Suzanne took off her sandals and put on her beach shoes.

"Oh beach shoes," said Dee. "That's a great idea. I should have bought some beach shoes. But I like to be in touch with the earth and the water, you know. So I can communicate without any barriers."

"Yeah," said Suzanne.

"Hey, look! There's the moon!"

Suzanne followed Dee's pointing finger. She was right. There was the moon, hanging like a disc of cloud in the blue sky.

"When the Lady Moon shows herself in the daytime, that's a real spiritual message," said Dee.

"Uh-huh," said Suzanne.

She surveyed the beach and picked up one of the stones that were scattered around her. It was smooth, warm, heavy, fitted well in the bowl of her hand.

"But with this house, I don't know. Her messages are complex. It's like getting the two tarot cards, the Moon and the Tower, combined. Do you understand?"

"Sure," said Dee. The stone in her hand felt perfect. Strange how she'd picked up exactly the right stone for her, just like Dee had said.

She walked down to where the water lapped up over her feet. She sighed. It was a shame. But Dee was right, there was something wrong with it. The place was sick with beauty. She could feel it now.

Dee came and stood beside her, as Suzanne knew she would.

"But when I did my cards last night, do you know I didn't get the Moon in there at all. You know what I got?"

"Death," said Suzanne.

"What?" Dee said. "How did you know that?"

"Look," said Suzanne. "Look at the moon's reflection in the water. You can see the house."

Dee leaned forward and was about to say something, but Suzanne shut her up by smashing the rock into the back of her thick head.

~

In the water taxi back to Lumbarda, Suzanne closed her eyes. This is a peaceful place, she thought. The sound of the engine cutting up the water was genuinely meditative. It almost washed away the sound of the wet crunch of Dee's skull collapsing into her brains, the splash and thunk of her body falling into the sea. Afterwards, Suzanne had picked her way around the rocks until she found another little cove where she could wash the blood off her hands and out of her hair. She'd swum for a while, then lay on the pebbles and tried to read her book, but the words kept melting off the page, so she dozed instead, under the weird moon which hovered in a cloudless blue sky. When she got back to the little jetty late in the afternoon, the taxi boat captain had greeted her in Croatian, and smiled at her, which made him look even more handsome. Really, everything was going perfectly.

Back at her hotel, she phoned Joe again. In a way, she'd have liked to tell him about today. He might have been proud of her. But more likely he wouldn't have understood, and anyway, he wasn't going to answer. Maybe she should head home early. She'd be worried about him, wouldn't she? But it might look suspicious, leaving so soon after Dee's disappearance. Would anyone notice Dee hadn't come back from her island jaunt? Suzanne thought lots of people would notice, but no one would care. Then she reprimanded herself. Don't be mean, Suzanne. No, it was better to stay on her holiday as planned. The longer she took to find Joe's body at the bottom of the stairs, the more doubt there would be about the time of death. She'd have to remember to call every day, and maybe call the kids too. But not yet – she didn't want to worry them.

The moon rose over the water, with its little house invisibly perched like a hat. Did I do the right thing, Suzanne asked the people in the house on the moon. Is this what you wanted? But the answer never came.

The Naughty House

We notice Emma's empty chair on Saturday morning. No one says anything about it, not even the teachers. But when Mrs Thing comes into the classroom, she marches right up to Emma's desk and peels off the sticker that says "eMMa" in glittery pink pen. She scrunches it up and it sticks to her fingers, and she says, "Oh fudge," but nobody laughs or says anything. Then we do our sums and spellings.

After that, it's playtime. The best time. Last week at playtime, Emma got the red car to play with, and Nathan got the blue truck. "I'm red, you're blue," Emma said to Nathan. "I'll race you." They pushed the cars over the floor back and forth, saying "Zoom zoom" and giggling, until Mrs Thing came in and pulled them apart. We're supposed to play quietly by ourselves at playtime. So they were both naughty, but only Emma's chair is empty.

After playtime, Mrs Thing makes us follow her to the top of the house, up all the stairs, and stand together in the attic. We think we're going to be punished and have to spend the night sleeping up here. It doesn't seem too bad, except for the spiders. Usually we have to sleep in the cellar if we're naughty, and all on our own, and there are rats in there, which are worse than spiders. Maybe Emma's been put in the cellar and they've forgotten about her. But somehow, we don't think so.

Mrs Thing stands aside and now we see an enormous telescope pointing out of the attic window. Mrs Thing says everyone should take turns to look through the telescope, but only using our one eye and we aren't allowed to touch anything with our hands. The telescope is pointed at the moon, and when we press our one eye to the lens, the moon appears very big and close, so close we can see craters and rocks. And on the moon, there is a house.

It's a tall, thin house, with a pointed roof. We can see tiny dark shadows that might be windows or doors. The house looks like it's made out of moon, like it's grown there, because it's the same colour as the moon: white and grey and silvery. It must be a big house for us to be able to see it from so far away, even through the telescope. But we don't have time to study it properly, because everyone has to have a turn.

After we've all looked, Mrs Thing makes us sit cross-legged on the floor. She says, "That house you just saw is called The Naughty House. It's a special place where children go if they are naughty. Because it's on the moon, it's very cold, and there's nothing to eat except moon porridge, which has rocks in it. And there are no kind mummies or daddies there who might come and adopt you. There are only rocks. Do you want to go to the Naughty House, children?"

"No, Miss," we say.

"That's right, of course you don't. And you won't be sent to the Naughty House as long as you're not naughty. Do you understand?"

"Yes, Miss," we say.

That night, after the house has gone dark and quiet and we're in bed, Nathan whispers, "Emma's in the Naughty House." We're all thinking it, but only Nathan has to say everything out loud.

When we go to sleep, we dream we are floating out of the windows and up into space. It's cold and dark but then the moon comes out, a ball of silver glitter, and we float in the sparkling rays of moonlight until morning.

~

Next Saturday, there's an empty chair where there should be Nathan. We guessed it would be him who got sent to the Naughty House, but we didn't say it because we didn't want to make it come true. We all know that Nathan has been naughty, though. He played cars with Emma, and he whispered after dark. And then, last week when we were supposed to be lined up nicely for the mummies and daddies to inspect us, Nathan had a shoelace undone and his hair was sticking up on his head like a hedgehog. Even though there was only one set of mummies and daddies that day, and they wanted a girl, Mrs Thing said it was still naughty of Nathan to have hedgehog hair.

Now, every night before bed, we have to go upstairs to the attic and look at the house on the moon, to remind ourselves to be good. We try to see Nathan and Emma through the windows in the Naughty House, but they must be too small and far away. We can't see anything through the rectangles of darkness. We wonder if they can look out of the windows and see the Earth.

We're all afraid of the Naughty House. All except Danny. He wants to go. He says he'll rescue Emma and Nathan and then they'll get a rocket back down to Earth and come and rescue us all too. This gets everyone very excited and we're all talking at once when Mrs Thing storms into the playroom. She can't tell who's started it, so we all get the standing-up punishment. We don't mind though. It's better to all be punished together. Maybe we can all go to the Naughty House together and then it won't be so bad. We can pick the rocks out of the porridge. Even after three hours, when our legs are in agony, and some of us have fallen, we still have a fizzy feeling in our heads, thinking about the moon and the house.

Also, it's alright because we know that it's going to be Danny next, and not one of us.

But we're wrong about that. It isn't Danny next. It's me.

~

In the beginning we think we have become darkness. We melt into it like ice. Our fingers are frozen and when we try to move them we find that they are gone, that we're trying to move darkness. We see only deep black space, space which invades our eyes, ears, nostrils, pores until we become the same substance as space, our bodies no longer bodies but scattered atoms rushing away from us.

We're ripped apart; we're ripped away. And when I come back together, I am an I. A lonely letter by myself. We are gone. And I am cold. I curl up around myself, shivering, teeth chattering, clenched around myself in the darkness. When at last I'm able to open my eyes, I see whiteness that is blinding. I feel a softness beneath me, a softness like earth, but I know it can't be earth. I know I'm on the moon.

~

Someone calls my name. It's the first time I've heard it, I think. I know I must have heard it before, but this is the first time I realise it applies to me. It's a woman's voice, calling me.

"Matty," she sings. "Wakey wakey, rise and shine!"

She's standing in the doorway and the white light is behind her so I can't see her features, only her shape. Hair that curls out at the bottom and a flared skirt. Hands on hips.

"He's awake," she says, turning her head away.

Another voice speaks. "About time."

"Oh dear, Father, don't be a grump! Or we'll have to send *you* to the Naughty House."

So it's true, I think. And a horrible feeling goes through my whole body. I am here and I am completely alone. I'm not sure which is worse.

~

The woman says I should call her Mother, because she is the Mother of the House. And she says I should call the man Father, because that makes us like a family. I follow her out of the little room and down the long corridor and through a door and down many steps until we come to a room with a dining table. There are two children sitting at the end of the table. I feel I can't breathe when I look at them. Like all the air has been pushed out of my body. It takes me several long moments to understand that I am looking at Emma and Nathan. And they are looking back at me.

"Go on," says Mother. "Go and join your little friends."

I run to them and they surround me and hold me. But it's not like before. We aren't all together anymore. Not properly.

"It's gone for me too," says Emma. "I think it's because of travelling through space."

"I don't remember anything about it," I say.

"Me either," says Nathan. "Maybe they drugged us."

I look down at the plate of food which has been put in front of me. It's not gruel, or porridge with rocks in. There's a big pile of broccoli and a slab of something pinkish-grey. I poke it with my fork. It's spongy, and my fork turns it to mush.

"Mystery meat," Nathan says.

"Weird," I say.

"At least you didn't have to be the first," says Emma. "I was all on my own until Nathan got here."

Her voice wavers in the middle of saying that. Poor Emma, I think. I'm so glad it wasn't me who went first.

"I don't even know what I did that was naughty," I say.

"I don't think this even is the Naughty House," says Nathan, pushing the pink meat around his plate. "They don't give us any punishments. All we do is play games and we eat three meals a day."

"And we have tests," Emma says. "But you don't have to do anything for them, just lie there."

"And lessons," I say.

"No," they say. "No lessons."

"I don't understand," I say.

"Well, dear," says Mother, who is suddenly standing behind me. "Ours is not to question why. Now eat up all your lovely dinner, won't you, and then you can play games before bed."

~

I don't like having a bedroom on my own. Nathan and Emma say I'll get used to it, but I don't think I ever will. The only good thing about my room is the window. It's just above my bed and I can sit in the corner hugging my pillow and looking out at space. I can see the Earth hanging there, shining like a bauble with blue and green patterns. It's so far away, I can't believe I'll ever get back there. Everyone I know on Earth is so incredibly tiny and distant that they almost don't exist. I push my finger against a wee red spider that crawls under the window, leaving a little smear on the wall. The people on Earth aren't even as big as that spider. They're not even specks.

~

When Danny arrives, I'm so happy to see him. I hug him and hold him tight, remembering how sad I was when I first got here. But Danny doesn't seem sad. He pushes us away from him and sits down at the table. He points at his plate and says, "What's this crap?"

Nathan giggles. Emma shushes him.

"Don't swear, Danny" she says. And to Nathan she says, "Stop being such a baby."

"It's just meat," I say. "Mystery meat."

"That's not meat," says Danny.

"Now Daniel," says Mother. She always lurks closely at dinnertime. "Don't be ungrateful. We can't always have everything we want, just the way we want it. We're on the moon, after all."

Danny frowns, screwing up his face. "Where's the porridge then," he mutters. But Mother doesn't hear him, or at least, she doesn't respond. Danny sits in front of his plate for a long time, staring, then shakes his head and folds his arms.

"It's alright, dear," says Mother. "You'll eat when you're hungry." She takes the plate away.

After dinner, we take Danny to the games room and show him all the things in there. The tennis ball, the cuddly dog with one ear, the pack of playing cards with most of them still in it, and best of all, a box that has six toy cars and two tiny dolls that can almost sit in the cars. Danny looks closely at everything, but doesn't want to play. He clears a space in the middle of the floor and sits cross-legged, looking serious. I remember what he said, before, when we all got in trouble and had to do the standing punishment.

"Danny," I say. "It's okay. We don't need to be rescued now. It's good here."

The others nod. We sit around Danny and pat his bony little knees.

"We get three meals a day," says Emma.

"You get used to the mystery meat," says Nathan. "It's not that bad."

"And there's no punishments," I say. "Well, only the tests."

"What tests?" Danny wants to know.

"It's nothing," says Emma. "We don't have to talk about it."

"You don't have to do them every day," Nathan says.

"The worst bit is the needle," I add.

Danny looks up at me. The other two look at the floor. Maybe I'm not supposed to mention the needles. Even Nathan didn't mention the needles, and he can never keep his mouth shut about anything. But Danny's going to find out soon enough.

"All it is," I tell him, "is you have to go into the test room and then Father comes in dressed like a doctor and he sticks a needle in your arm. Then nothing else happens and you wake up in your room."

Danny looks between the three of us, seeking confirmation.

"I don't like it," he says.

"It's okay," said Emma. "You don't really feel anything."

"You feel really sick when you wake up but it goes away," says Nathan.

Emma tuts. "It's only in the mornings," she says. "You can do whatever you want the rest of the time."

"No," says Danny. "I don't like needles. I'm not going to do it."

- 42 -

"You have to," I say. "You'll get in trouble."

Danny laughs, but it's more like a dog's bark than a laugh. "I'm already in the Naughty House," he says. "How much worse can it get?"

~

I hear Danny's screams the next day when they take him for his test. I sit on my bed with my knees pulled up to my chest and I try to send Danny messages with my mind, like we all used to do in the home. Did we really do that? I'm not sure any more. Everything is so different now. Still, I keep trying. It's okay, I tell him. Don't be afraid. It'll be over soon.

He screams and bellows like an animal. I didn't know he could make those kinds of noises. It goes on for a long time, too, until eventually there's the sound of metal crashing and then silence. Tears prickle my eyes. Poor Danny. But the worst bit is over now.

At dinnertime he's silent and once again he refuses to eat. This time, Mother doesn't take the plate away. She stands over him and says, "One bite, Danny. One bite and you can get down from the table." But Danny sits with his arms folded and his lips pressed tightly together. Mother cuts up the meat into tiny pieces and puts one on the end of a fork. She holds the fork to Danny's lips, but he turns his head away.

The three of us are staring at Danny, not knowing what to do to help. Mother looks over at us and snaps, "You can go."

I don't want to leave Danny there, but what can I do? Me, Nathan and Emma walk together to the games room. Nathan empties the box of cars onto the floor. It all looks a bit rubbish in the games room now, after seeing Danny's reaction to it. I thought it was so good, such riches, but now I see it's just a few pathetic broken toys. Even the pack of cards has some missing.

Emma picks up one of the tiny people dolls. "It's broken," she says.

Nathan pats her on the shoulder. "It's fine," he says. "Danny's just a troublemaker."

We hear a shout from the dining room, and the sound of a plate smashing on the floor.

"Maybe they'll send him back," I say.

But a few minutes later, Danny appears in the games room. We all scramble up and gather around him.

"What happened?"

"Nothing," he says. He sits down on the floor and puts his head in his hands. "They made me eat it," he says.

I put a hand on his shoulder. He's thin and bony. He needs to eat.

"It wasn't so bad," he says. "I only had one bite."

I feel relieved, but at the same time I'm sad for Danny that he lost, even though I don't know why he wanted to win. I've never even thought about not eating before now. It's food and there's lots of it, that's all I know. In the home, there was never quite enough food, and we'd been hungry all the time. I'm not hungry here. But I have a creeping feeling that Danny was right to refuse to eat, and right to refuse the needles, too. I wish it had occurred to me to refuse it all.

"You'll get used to it, Danny," says Nathan. "You don't have to make a big deal out of everything."

Danny kicks a car across the room. "I don't want to get used to it! I don't want to be like you, you stupid... lump."

Nathan throws himself on top of Danny and starts screaming in his ear while trying to punch him in the side. Danny fights back and within seconds they're a blur of arms and legs, punching and kicking and pulling each other's hair. Emma and I circle them, lunging in to try to pull them apart without getting drawn in to the violence. Then Mother appears in the doorway, with Father behind her.

"What in heaven's name do you think you're doing?" Mother strides right into the room and grabs each boy by an ear, prising them apart. They are both red-faced, tear-stained, angry messes.

Father surveys them from the doorway. "I told you, Mother," he says. "This won't do at all."

"He's a naughty child," she says, still holding Danny by the ear. She's let go of Nathan, who is rubbing his face and looking like he's trying not to cry any more. "But if he wasn't naughty, he wouldn't be here in the first place, would he, Father?"

Father sighs. His eyes are kind of blank, which is what makes him so frightening, I realise. His eyes are dead. "We'll talk about this later, Mother." He turns and leaves the room.

Mother lets go of Danny at last. "I don't want to know how this started," she says. "As far as I'm concerned, you are all equally to blame. Any more nonsense like this and I'll... you'll be... Well, let's just say there *will* be consequences and you *won't* like them. Understood?"

We all nod and look down at our feet. Except Danny. Danny rubs his sore ear and stares at Mother.

"What can you do," he says, in a tone of wonder. "What can you actually do?"

"I don't want to hear another peep out of you, Daniel," Mother says. "All of you, get to bed. Danny, you sleep in Matty's room tonight. Matty, you'll keep an eye on Danny and make sure he doesn't get into any more trouble."

"Yes, Mother," I say, flushing with pleasure at the thought of sharing my room with someone. I hate sleeping alone and I've had bad dreams since I got here, dreams of falling endlessly through lonely space. But now I'll have Danny with me. I can't help grinning. Danny scowls at me and I feel ashamed. I'm on *your* side, I try to tell him in my mind. But I can tell my messages aren't getting through.

That night, we don't sleep. Danny paces up and down the tiny room, while I sit on the bed, hugging my knees.

"I don't get it," Danny keeps saying. "It doesn't make sense. This is the Naughty House but we don't get any punishments here. We don't have to eat porridge with rocks in it."

"That's only what Mrs Thing said, though," I interrupt him. "She's never been here so how would she know?"

"And that's another thing," Danny says. "How did we even get here? And where does the food come from? There's no animals here, are there? So what are we eating?"

I think about it for a moment. "Like... Spam?" I say.

Danny grunts, non-committal.

"I bet it's some kind of Spam and they've got thousands of tins of it somewhere," I say.

"Okay," says Danny. "But what are the tests for?"

That, I can't answer. It isn't that I haven't thought about it – I have, of course. But only in a distracted, floaty kind of a way. I've never *really* thought about it. I've checked my body in the shower, looking for marks and bruises that they might have given me during the tests. Sometimes I'm sore in different places. But that has always happened, even back in the home.

"Are they even human?" Danny asks now. "Have you seen their eyes? Mother and Father... are they aliens? Have we been abducted by aliens?"

I don't say anything. I don't have any of the answers Danny wants. Up until he arrived, I didn't even have any of the questions. I wonder at myself, now. How am I so passive, so accepting? Always quietly going along with everything I'm told, doing what everyone else does. The worst thing that has ever happened to me, I remind myself, is being torn away from the group and forced to be alone in my own mind. It's terrible and every moment I'm wishing I could merge my mind with another's again. Go back to when it was *us*, when it was better. Wouldn't Danny like it better, too? But he is still pacing, still thinking, wide awake and muttering under his breath.

"Let's get some sleep," I say, patting the bed. "It'll be morning soon."

Danny whirls around to face me. "And *that's* the strangest thing of all," he says. But before he can say more, the bedroom door opens and Father stands in the doorway. His big body fills the frame. He has on his doctor costume.

"Come with me, Daniel," he says.

"No," says Danny. "You can't make me."

But of course Father can make him. And he does. He reaches into the room and picks Danny up by the scruff of his neck, and drags him away. I hear his screams for a long time, even though I have my hands over my ears and I'm humming loudly to myself, rocking back and forth in the bed.

After what seems like a very long time, the screaming stops, and some time after that Mother comes to the open door.

"Wakey wakey, rise and shine!" she sings into the room.

And that's the strangest thing of all. I hear Danny's voice echoing in my mind. What did he mean, I wonder. What is the strangest thing? Will he be able to stay in my room again tonight, and tell me what the strangest thing is? But do I even want him back in my room now? The truth is, I've begun to feel afraid of Danny. I have a horrible feeling that he's going to get us all into a lot of trouble.

~

Danny isn't there at dinnertime. Emma and Nathan don't say anything about it and neither do I, but I'm wishing very hard that Danny will come back. He's the only one of us who has any heart, I see that now. The only one with courage. Him not being there makes me think about when Emma's chair had been empty on that Saturday morning, when we'd all been so afraid. I suppose the others who are still down there on Earth will be looking up at us through the telescope in the attic now. Trying to see us through the windows. But we are too far away.

And I remember we couldn't even always see the house on the moon at all, because the moon has an orbit, it goes around the Earth and sometimes the Earth hides it from the sun, so you can't always see the whole thing. Mrs Thing taught us that in science.

And that's the strangest thing of all...

Mother stands behind my chair, interrupting my train of thought.

"I want you to know, dear children," she begins, "that there is nothing to be afraid of here." She pauses, and I feel her hand grip my shoulder and squeeze. "There's nothing to be afraid of – *if* you are good children. But if you are bad children, then I'm sorry to say that you'll be sent to the *Very* Naughty House. In the *Very* Naughty House, there's no lovely meals like this one. There's nothing to eat but porridge with rocks in it. Do you want to go to the *Very* Naughty House, children?"

"No, Mother," we chant in unison.

"And you won't," says Mother. "As long as you're good."

~

"Danny's in the Very Naughty House," Nathan whispers.

We are in the games room, listlessly pushing the cars around the floor.

"Shut up, Nathan, you bigmouth" says Emma.

"You shut up, Miss Perfect Pants," Nathan says.

I bite my lip, wondering whether to tell them about the things Danny said to me, and how Father took him away, how he screamed and screamed. *And that's the strangest thing of all...* He'd been looking up at the window. Had he even pointed? He might have done.

There's a window in the games room. It's high up in the middle of the wall, too high to look out of, but I have an idea.

"Give me a leg up," I say.

Nathan flings his toy car away and scrambles towards me. Emma stands up, too. They intertwine their hands so I can stand on them and they boost me towards the window. I grab the vertical iron bars. It's the same view as from my window. The thin, black, frightening empty space. And the Earth glowing blue and green in the midst of the darkness. It's exactly the same view. And that's the strangest thing of all, I think. It really is strange.

"My arm's hurting," says Nathan.

"One minute," I say. "Give me a bit more height."

They groan, but boost me a few centimetres higher. I step from their hands and place my feet against the wall so I can haul myself up level with the window and push an arm between the bars, reaching out towards space. Reaching out into space, and touching... something solid.

"Get down from there!"

Father's voice booms through the room and I let go of the bars and fall backwards to the floor, landing on one of Nathan's discarded toy cars, right in the small of my back. Emma screams. Hot tears flood my eyes, and I try to hold them back but the pain is too sharp and I can feel the coldness under my skin where it's broken and the blood is running out.

Mother's face looms over me. From this angle, she looks alien and monstrous, and I wonder why I haven't seen it before. I should have been afraid, I realise. All this time, I should have been terrified. But I haven't been. Until Danny came, I'd been nothing. Not scared, not angry, not even sad really. Just nothing.

But it's all different now.

"It's not real," I say. My voice comes out as a croak. I don't know if Nathan and Emma hear me, so I speak louder. I shout. "It's not real," I shout. "We're not on the moon. We're not naughty. None of it is real."

Father has me by the arms and he's dragging me out of the games room. The pain sears through my body and I start screaming. It feels good to scream, to let the pain and terror roar out through my mouth. I scream and scream as Father drags me along the corridor. I understand now, why Danny kept screaming. Why he kept screaming, right up until the very end.

All Too Red

A champagne cork popped unexpectedly, and everyone laughed. Being famous was like an endless birthday party. High as the sky, blowing out candles that instantly re-lit themselves, unwrapping present after present until the floor of the private jet was covered in boxes and tissue paper, and the stewardess came in discreetly to sweep everything away. Fame made people crazy and careless – careless like Gatsby, uplifted by champagne bubbles until they were floating way above the heads of everyone else. All those heads, looking up. Waiting for her to fall and shatter.

But Baker Fleet was not about to shatter. She was hard and happy, spinning up there in her metal balloon. Fearless. Untouchable. The sky roared past her, around the sleek fat little jet that was hers alone. She felt good. The interview had been word-perfect, and Jimmy had gifted her a cute silver knife small enough to slide into a purse. The handle was engraved with the title of her biggest hit, *Heart Like a Knife*, and the phases of the moon, and the blade folded into the handle. Neat. And the performance had been amazing. The audience had been beside itself, fainting and sobbing as it fought through itself, reaching for her; the crowd like a thousand-limbed goddess, seeking her touch, her look, her grace. They loved her, and their love created an ecstatic energy that was practically supernatural. It was brilliantly frightening. Baker thought that if she ever fell, she wouldn't shatter. Instead she'd be torn to pieces by the divine, chaotic mouths of her fans. They'd eat her alive.

She tried to hold on to that feeling, knowing it would soon be gone. All that energy, gone. Dissipated, dissolved into the frigid air-conditioned spaces of her Los Angeles house, where she would slink around like a hunger.

Heather lurched towards her across the aisle and put a glass of champagne in her hand.

"You were so great," Heather gushed, her eyes wide, conveying sincerity, which Baker knew was bullshit. Heather always treated Baker like she was a situation that needed to be handled. Baker smiled, a brief thin smile, resenting her for the compliment. Somehow it undermined everything Baker was feeling and made it all seem ordinary. Words did that: they obscured and disguised and put fences around things. The only word Baker needed to hear was her own name, chanted over and over. She drained the champagne glass and closed her eyes, luxuriating in the echoes. But Heather wasn't finished.

"Hold on, hon. One sec. I've got Max."

Baker opened her hand for the phone and lazily brought it to her ear.

"Tell me you've got good news, Max."

"The best, kiddo! You nailed it. We're in. We're going to the moon!"

~

"How do you feel about having the official soundtrack to the House on the Moon expedition?" Jimmy leaned back, opening his arms expansively, inviting the studio audience to cheer. They nearly took the roof off.

Baker laughed, and put her hands to her heart. "You guys..." she said, and waited for the applause to die down before answering Jimmy's question. "It's an incredible privilege. Like, I sometimes have to catch my breath and think, is this really happening?"

"And what about the song? What can we expect?"

"Ah come on, Jimmy," she laughed. "You know I can't tell you that. What I can say is that I'm going to do my best to live up to the moment. You guys know that, right?" She turned to the audience, lifted her hands in supplication. They cheered in response.

"Okay, but can you tell us if it's a love song?"

Baker laughed. "Is there any other kind? Listen, I'm kind of a dork, you know? I sing about falling in love and, well, falling out of love." She shrugged and made a face, faux-apologetic. "Which I, unfortunately, know all about," she quipped. Roars of laughter from the audience. They were loving this. "But seriously, this is a song for, like, literally everyone."

Jimmy leaned forward conspiratorially. "You're known for your incredible lyrics. But some people are worried that your words are not always as wholesome as they should be."

Baker frowned. "I don't..."

Jimmy held up a hand. "Can you tell us what you were trying to say here?" He picked up his sheaf of papers, cleared his throat and read, "And if he doesn't love me anymore, I'll cut off his head and send it through the mail to his fucking whore."

Gales of laughter erupted from the crowd. Jimmy Fallon slumped over his chair, as though someone had shot him in the chest. He was laughing. Everyone was laughing. Was it supposed to be a joke?

"I didn't write that," Baker said. "That's horrible." But no one was listening. She looked round the studio, desperately seeking Heather, Max, anyone on her team, anyone who could come and rescue her. But there was no one. There was only the terrible laughter, and then she was awake, and the sound of the jet engine was throbbing in her ears, champagne bubbles dribbling from her open mouth.

"Fuck," she said. Times like this, she wanted to fire her own brain. It's me, I'm the problem, she thought. If anyone else acted that way towards her, she'd can them before they could blink. Even Doctor Lumna couldn't help. She kept trying her on different medications to stop the nightmares, but nothing worked. Somehow, the fucked up part of her brain always managed to get a message through. She'd been having these awful dreams ever since she'd seen the house on the moon. She'd read on the internet that other people were having them too: Moonmares, they called them. But Doctor Lumna said that 'moonmares' weren't a thing. Maybe she should fire Doctor Lumna.

She checked the time on her phone. They'd be landing soon. She'd call Callum from the car. At least there was him: simple, handsome Callum. She couldn't wait to tell him the news about the moon gig. He wouldn't like it at all. He'd be jealous as hell.

~

It was two in the morning, Los Angeles time, but Baker wasn't ready to go to bed, not even with Callum waiting in it for her. It occurred to her that it was time to break up with him. She ought to be single now, so she could meet an astronaut and fall in love with him instead. Write not just a moon song, but a whole space album. That would be something. The press would eat that up. *Space Fleet: Baker's new romance is stratospheric!* That kind of thing.

She slid over the tiled floors in her socks, chasing her cats. She tried to pick them up and pet them, but they yowled and slunk away from her. They never liked her energy after she'd done a late-night talk show. Maybe they thought she was selling out.

Restless, she sat at the piano for a while, trying out some melodies. What kind of song should she write for the House on the Moon? Something cosmic, something dreamy. But her dreams these days were gruesome, blood-filled. Red moon, she thought. Blood moon... But remember, this isn't some bonus track or B-side. This song is going to be played on the actual fucking moon. Baker was used to being under pressure; she thrived on it, in fact. But this was intense. This was something no one had ever done before. I'm a pioneer, she thought. She touched a few piano keys, finding a melody under the word *pioneer*. Maybe? It was a start, anyway.

She recorded a voice note to herself. She ought to sleep now, because the next few weeks were going to be packed with meetings and press and she didn't want to look fat and ugly in the photos. But that's what make-up was for, she told herself. And instead of going to bed, she went to the top of the house and onto the roof, where she kept her telescope. It was a huge one, good enough for a professional astronomer, or so she'd been told. And some English astrophysicist, Brian someone, had sent her a copy of his book, but she hadn't got around to reading it yet. She liked to tell interviewers that she'd been an amateur astronomer all her life – it came up in all those 'Ten Reasons Why Baker Fleet Is A Boss Bitch' articles now – but it wasn't true. Like everyone else, she'd just wanted to see the house on the moon.

She wanted to see it now. There was something compelling about it, almost addictive. Baker felt something like disappointment that other people were allowed to look at it too. Usually when she liked something, she could have it all to herself. But she had to share the house with everyone and that made her anxious. What if someone else wrote the best song about it? What if someone else figured out its mystery before she did? What would become of her, if she lost her novelty? But when she put her eye to the lens, she felt calm. The house was there, like it always was, as if it had been there forever. Finally, she felt she could breathe. She decided to go and wake Callum up, see the look on his face when she told him she was about to become richer and more famous than even her wildest dreams.

~

The lights were off in the bedroom. Baker stepped carefully through shadows towards the bed. She could make out a patch of darkness that must have been Callum's body, and she stretched out a hand to touch him. His leg, his flank. He didn't stir. She climbed up on the bed and straddled his body.

"Hey babe," she said. "My flight was awful, thanks for asking."

She leaned forward to kiss him, kissed his neck, maybe, no it was his mouth, wet and open. But he didn't respond.

Baker leaned back and clapped her hands to turn the lights on. And screamed.

Callum was sprawled beneath her. His mouth was hanging open, his head turned to the side. It lolled there, looking awkward, hanging off the mess where his neck had been hacked into. There was blood everywhere. All over Baker, too. On her mouth, where she'd kissed him.

She stopped screaming when she heard footsteps in the corridor. Jumped up and locked the bedroom door. She yelled, "No, I'm okay, don't come in. Get Max. I need Max."

There was blood on the doors now, and on the cream carpet and even on one of the paintings hanging on the wall, a portrait of Baker and her cats. She loved that painting. Had the blood come from her or was it there already? Whoever killed Callum must have left a trail of blood through the house, surely? But how could it happen? There were bodyguards everywhere. Cameras everywhere. The thought struck her: was this a mistake? Was it supposed to have been *her*?

She was sitting at the foot of the bed when Max arrived. Holding her new silver knife in both hands. Still shaking. Max sat beside her.

"Baker," he said. "What are we going to do with you?"

"It was real, Max, I swear," she pleaded. "There was blood... it was everywhere. It was awful."

"Callum's in London. You want to talk to him?"

"No, it's okay." London? Had he even told her he was in London? Baker felt blindsided by this information. He was cheating on her, wasn't he? For a second, she almost wished that his violent death wasn't just a hallucination.

"Calm down, kid. Let's call the doc and get you some sleep."

"You believe me, don't you Max?"

"Oh hell, Baker, come on. Don't ask me that. How can I believe you? There's nothing here. No body, no crime."

"I know that!" Baker cried. "But that makes it worse! Don't you see?"

Max patted her back. "It's the pressure," he said. "You're overwhelmed, kid."

"It's not the pressure. It's not that, Max. It's the moon. It's fucking with me."

Max sighed. "You can't do this to Elon, okay? Not to mention, well, fucking *everything*. If you fuck this up then Baker Fleet is over. Hashtag-Baker-Fleet-is-over. You want that, kid?"

"Don't call me kid," she muttered.

"No one will be calling you, period, unless you get your shit together, kiddo."

Baker was quiet for a moment, letting that sink in.

"What would you have done," Baker asked, "if it was real? What would happen to me? The press would go crazy, wouldn't they? It would be awful."

"The press would never get to hear of it, kid. I'd cover that shit up good. I'm your ride or die, remember? Bury the bodies and all that."

"That's weirdly reassuring," Baker said. It was good to be reminded that Max would always be there to fix whatever problems came her way. "What would I do without you, Max?"

"You'd be in deep shit, kiddo," he replied.

~

Doctor Lumna put Baker on some new drugs, not sleeping pills but something psychiatric, the name of which Baker could never remember. They made her want to eat, which she hadn't been planning to do until after the moon launch. She was constantly ravenous and woke up in the middle of the night to go to the kitchen and raid the fridge, and sit on the floor remembering midnights when she and Callum had danced in the kitchen, by the light of the refrigerator. It hurt to remember. She missed Callum. He'd broken up with her after her meltdown – he'd used it as his reason for breaking up with her. Said he couldn't handle it if anything bad happened to her when he wasn't around. Baker knew that what he really couldn't handle was her being more famous and successful than him. He was already in the papers, out and about with some other girl.

Fuck it, she thought, stuffing cookie dough into her mouth. I'm going to date an astronaut, anyway.

She'd been secretly auditioning them for a while now, watching them on television, hanging around at SpaceX with Elon. There was one she liked, Mike. She'd never dated a Mike before. It was a good, wholesome American name, she thought. Plus it rhymed with a lot of words. Not that she'd be so crass as to put anyone's actual name in a song, at least not these days. Bartholomew padded over and pushed his head into Baker's hand. "Hey Mew," she said, and fed him a tiny pinch of cookie dough. He climbed onto her lap where he started purring. She watched his soft belly rise and fall and thought about plunging her little silver knife between his ribs and ripping him open. A horrible thought.

She took the knife with her everywhere now, ever since the moonmare about Callum. It made her feel safer, just to have it. Doctor Lumna said that was okay. It was okay to have a talisman, even if what you were guarding against was your own dreams.

"See, Mew," Baker said, "I'm sane now."

~

"I can't believe I finally get to meet you," said Mike the astronaut. "I'm a huge fan! I'm a Fleety!" Baker thanked him and rolled her eyes. She'd already been mildly disappointed to realise that Mike was short for Mikhail and rather than being all-American, he was actually from Ukraine. Now she found out he was a fan and that made her uncomfortable. Her fans were crazy. But she supposed it would make it easy to seduce him. And thank God it was the Ukraine he was from and not Russia. She'd get social media credit for dating a Ukrainian, surely? With the war or whatever it was going on over there? Anyway, he was so tall, and handsome as hell. Those eyes. Damn, she'd never seen that colour blue. She pulled him towards her for a selfie.

"My instagram's gonna blow up," he said. "Oh hey, there's Elon."

Shit. Baker laughed as though Mike had said something funny, and manoeuvred around him so she could keep an eye on Elon. She really didn't want to get into a conversation about the song. She wasn't ready to talk about it yet. Because the song wasn't ready yet. The truth was, she had nothing.

Don't think about it, she told herself. But the panic was already flooding through her veins.

"Are you okay?" Mike put a meaty hand on her shoulder. He was proportioned like a Disney prince, huge hands and bulging shoulders. Baker tried to think about his abs. Tried to imagine them rippling under his expensive white shirt.

But all she could think about was the fact that she still didn't have an idea for a song and if she didn't come up with something soon, her career was over. Her life was over.

"Hey," said Mike. "Take a deep breath."

Baker breathed. It was the drugs, she thought. Those horrible little pills the doctor had given her. They were messing with her creativity. She had to stop taking them. They were making her fat, too. No one could see it yet, but Baker could feel it. Even if she came up with the best song in the world, her career would be over as soon as she gained ten pounds.

She breathed out and smiled at Mike. "I'm so sorry," she said. "I'm fine, really." She grabbed two glasses of champagne from a passing waiter and handed one to Mike. "Come up to the roof with me," she said. It wasn't really a question.

"I heard you're an amateur astronomer," said Mike, as they stepped onto the roof and headed towards the telescope. "I'm impressed."

"Really? You heard that? I've always been so fascinated by the solar system," said Baker. "I'm so glad you knew that about me. People usually think I'm shallow because of... well, because of all this."

Mike laughed. "No one thinks you're shallow," he said. "I know there's a lot to you. A lot to... devour."

Something about the way he said that made her feel uncomfortable. She didn't like that kind of talk. She turned away so he couldn't see her expression, and put her eye to the lens of the telescope. There was the house – her house – perched like a little hat over the moon's inscrutable face. It made her feel good. It made her feel better. She knew that Mike was standing right behind her. She could sense him as though he were a wild animal. In a moment, she would turn around, and he would kiss her, and it would all begin, exactly as she'd planned. But she kept looking at the moon, letting it flood her with light. Inspire me, she thought. It was more of a prayer than a thought. She sent her plea into the universe.

And then she turned around.

The astronaut smiled. His teeth were white and sparkled. They were going to look so good together in the photographs, Baker thought. Everything was going to be okay.

"Baker? You're having a nightmare. Wake up."

The astronaut was whispering to her, shaking her shoulder, but she couldn't see him. She saw his suit, but behind the dome of his visor was a skeleton, hung with strips of flesh, eyeballs dangling inside the cage of his skull.

She screamed.

Mike shook her shoulder. "Baker, wake up, wake up. You're dreaming."

She opened her eyes and thanked God it was him this time, her blessed astronaut, holding her in his strong arms. She breathed into his neck, taking in the smell of him, the smell of space rocks and nothing.

"Why are you wearing your spacesuit?" she asked.

His answer was the wet sound of stabbing flesh, the gurgle of blood.

Baker woke up. She clapped her hands for the light and it came on. Mike was lying beside her, fast asleep. He slept through everything, said it was an important skill for an astronaut to have. But she needed him, she thought. They'd only just met and already he was letting her down. Why were men like this, she wondered. Oblivious. Selfish. *Ugh*. She pushed his shoulder, said "Wake up!" He didn't stir. She pushed again and again, until he finally rolled away from her, and she saw the void where his face was supposed to be.

She struggled to get out of the dream, to wake up, finally wrenching her eyes open and turning on the lights. Her eyes blurred. Heart hammered. She felt sweaty and shaky from the nightmare, and thought about calling Doctor Lumna. It was three in the morning, but why should the useless doctor sleep when Baker was suffering? But then she'd have to come over, and there'd be some fucking bullshit about meditating and she'd have to sit through that just to get the sleeping pills and besides, it wasn't sleeping pills she needed. It was don't-have-nightmares pills. And she already knew Doctor

Lumna had nothing of that sort to hand. No way was Baker going back on the fat-and-uglies. She was just going to have to sweat this one out.

She wasn't completely sure that she was awake. But there was no astronaut in the bed beside her, and when the light came on it stayed on, and her heart was beginning to slow down.

Baker got out of bed, pulled on a jumper and went to the music room. She sat at the piano and picked out a melody, hoping for her fingers to stop shaking. The melody was interesting, she thought. Was it futuristic but also engaging, she wondered? She had Elon's cell phone number, should she call him and ask? Nah, what the fuck did he know about writing songs? Beside, he'd only start freaking out that it wasn't ready yet. She just had to chill. It wasn't like she'd never written a song before. She was putting too much pressure on it. That was the problem.

She took some deep breaths.

Pioneers. That was the only idea she'd had so far. She fingered the piano and whisper-sang some words. *I wanna be the first woman in space... the first one to rip off your face... tear your flesh from the bones and throw you into the wastes... of space.*

What. The. Fuck.

Where had that come from? Baker shook her head, took a deep breath. Try again.

If I'm the first woman in space, I'm gonna look down at the earth in your eyes, and I'm gonna...

She thumped the piano keys. "Fuck!" That was even worse.

She picked up her cell and called Max.

"Can we pay someone to write this?" She asked when Max finally answered the phone, groggy with sleep. "You think we can get a ghostwriter?"

"What are you talking about, kid?" Max sniffed, and suddenly sounded wide awake. "Come on, baby Bakes. You've got this. You're the best in the biz. You're Baker Fleet!"

"I can't do it, Max. I'm all in my head. I can't get anything out... I can't do it."

"There's no can't, Baker."

She knew she was in trouble when he addressed her by her actual name.

"Max, I'm sorry, but you don't know what it's been like. I've been trying so hard. It's just... it's gone." She felt tears prickling the backs of her eyes. What if it really was gone? What if she couldn't write anything again?

"I know what you need." It wasn't Max who had spoken, but the astronaut. He was standing in the doorway of her music room, filling it with his Disney frame.

Max was saying something to her, but she interrupted him. "You're right, Max, okay? It's okay. I'll figure it out. I'm going to figure it out and I'm going to call you in the morning." She ended the call.

"How did you get in?" she asked Mike.

"I never left," he said. "I fell asleep on the roof, waiting for you to come back."

"Oh." She felt bad. She'd forgotten all about him. "So what do I need?"

He grinned. "Some perspective."

"Okay," she said. "Let me just grab my purse."

~

The sky over Los Angeles was thick with smog. Mike drove fast, the Bugatti barely touching the tarmac as they sped up into the hills. "You're gonna love it," he said. "No cameras, no bodyguards. It's just me and you, babe."

Baker smiled and curled around herself in her seat. The astronaut was right. She already felt better for getting away from the house. She should have done this ages ago. She remembered when she was just starting out, driving on nights like this, trying to clear her head from all the noise so her music could break through. It had worked back then. Maybe it would work now.

Something was working, she thought. The higher they went in the hills, the clearer the night sky became. She could see the moon now, big and bloody, hanging over the fog of night.

"Blood moon," said the astronaut. "Isn't she pretty?"

"I wish I could see the house," said Baker. Would it be red, like the moon?

"You're going to love this," said the astronaut. "I'm going to blow your mind, babe."

Okay, thought Baker. But make it quick because I'm more interested in getting a song written. Sex with the astronaut sounded okay, but nothing was going to beat the thrill of having the first inter-galactic hit single. She patted his thigh. "I can't wait," she said.

He drove them to an unprepossessing, low building at the top of a scrubby hill. Parked outside and they jogged to the entrance, where he pressed his hand against the door to open it. "Biometrics," he said. "I've got full clearance."

"Nice," said Baker, wondering if it really was. The place didn't look like anything special, if she was honest. They jogged down a long walkway that seemed to curve and bend back on itself. Baker wasn't sure if it was her imagination, or whether they were actually climbing higher. She could feel the sweat beginning to break at the small of her back. Gross. If she wanted to go for a jog she had a whole gym in her house. Then they came to another door.

It opened into a giant silver hangar with a great glass dome covering it, and in the middle, an enormous contraption that Baker recognised as the controls of a huge telescope.

"Guess what, Baker," said Mike. "With this baby, you can see *through* the fucking windows."

"Oh my God. Are you serious?"

"You can see right inside the house. You wanna see?"

"You know I do!"

"Yeah, I know," said the astronaut. "But what's in it for me?"

Oh, that? How completely lame. Baker rolled her eyes and didn't even try to hide it. "Mike, seriously? We haven't even been on a proper date."

"But I love you," said Mike, and a massive grin spread over his face. "I can't stand how much I love you."

He lurched towards her and Baker lurched away. There was no surprise, not really. In a way, she reflected, she'd always known it would come to this. Her mind flashed back to their first meeting. She'd known he was trouble when he walked in – before that, even. Shame on her for not trusting her instincts. Or was it her fault? Had she invited it, by staring too much at the moon? Her thoughts spiralled, but he was on top of her already, tearing at her, trying to bite into her flesh. "I love you," he said. "I just love you so much."

"That's okay, baby," she crooned. "It's okay." She thrashed away from his chomping teeth, his churning mouth and clawing hands. It was okay, it really was. She could hear music, a melody, a bassline. Yes, it was here. Her inspiration was here. It gave her a surge of power. She kept moving, wriggling and squirming away from the astronaut's hungry mouth, and towards her purse that had snapped when he'd lunged at her. Her silver knife was in there, her talisman against dreams. It would work against flesh too. She scrabbled around with her hand until she had it, flicked it open, and plunged it deep into Mike's neck. With a few deft kicks she was out from under him, and now she could really go to town. She remembered how Callum had looked to her, his head hanging off his neck. It was good.

She tried to recreate it but really she needed a bigger knife. Even so, there was a lot of blood. It kept spurting out everywhere. Astronaut blood. Now we've got bad blood, Baker thought. She laughed at her own pun. She didn't really have any hard feelings towards the astronaut. If anything, she was grateful to him for giving her what she wanted. This was the real thing, wasn't it? It was real, no dream or nightmare. No other man had even come close to making her feel this way. The melody to her song was revolving around her head as she worked. She started humming it to herself. It was good.

She had to cut off Mike's hand to get out of the building, and that was annoying. The knife was sharp enough but it couldn't cut through bone and in the end she had to stand on his wrist and wrench the hand off his arm. Messy. And then there was the problem of the hand not being with his body, but how else was she supposed to get out of there? She needed his hand to open the doors. Her skin and hair would be under his nails, too, but that didn't prove anything. They were lovers, after all. And she did love him, really she did, despite his plasticky smile and fake tan and the fact that he'd tried to eat her. It didn't matter. It all paled in comparison with what he'd given her. Because the words to her song were coming now too, tumbling over the melody, something about the bloodlit night and the windows in the house on the moon. It was good. It was going to be everything Elon wanted. It was going to be epic. She was going to sing it live on the fucking moon, and nothing else really mattered.

She sat in Mike's Bugatti for half an hour, making voice notes on her phone. She got it, all of it, the whole song. When she was done, she looked up and the sky was beginning to get light. The astronaut's hand lay on the passenger seat, blood congealing on the leather. Gross.

She sent the voice notes to her cloud and copied Max in. Then as the red moon started to blur and melt across the sky, she got out of the car and called Max.

"I've got good news and bad news," she said. "Which do you want first?"

She looked up at the moon sinking below the horizon. Look what you made me do, she thought. Look what you made me do.

In Real Life

"It's not real," Zoran says. He jabs a finger towards his computer screen. "Look, there's an article by a NASA scientist. He's been sacked from his job for speaking out."

I don't look at his computer screen. I'm staring at the back of his head, wondering what's going on in there. This has been his refrain for the last few weeks. It's not real. None of it is real. It's a hoax.

"I've seen it with my own eyes," I say.

"No," he says, "you've seen it through a telescope."

"That I looked through with my own eyes."

"That's not the same thing."

This is like the birds, I think. Zoran got covid last spring, and moved into the spare room for a fortnight, and I left meals outside the door, and wiped everything down with antibacterial spray, and called him on the phone from the living room to tell him I loved him. After he came out of that quarantine, groggy and fogged over, he went out into the garden to see the sun. I watched him from the kitchen window, crouching down on the path. A few minutes later, he came into the flat with a dead sparrow in his hands, its entrails pooled in his palms.

"Look at this," he'd said. He showed me there was a tiny plastic chip in the mess of its stomach, like one of those little sim cards for a phone. Eating that was probably what had killed it, I thought. But Zoran didn't think so. He went straight to the internet and an hour later, he told me that birds weren't real. They were surveillance drones, he said, modelled to look like birds. Not all the birds, but that's the problem, he said. We don't know which ones are real and which are the ones that are spying on us. They perch on power lines to recharge themselves, he said. When I asked him why the dead sparrow didn't have a camera, only a plastic computer chip, he said that I was asking the wrong questions.

Now it was this. The house on the moon. Strange and extraordinary, but I'd seen it myself. I'd gone to the observatory at Blackford Hill, paid my money, stood in line, and had my four minutes with the telescope. I saw the house, and I even saw that it had windows, and the woman looking after the telescope told me that they had even more powerful telescopes able to see through the windows but so far there was only darkness inside.

Zoran didn't come with me that evening. If he had, maybe he would have been able to believe in it.

"This is just like the birds," I say.

"I was right about the birds," says Zoran.

"You really weren't."

I ask him how long he thinks I'm going to put up with this crap. But I only ask him in my head, because I'm scared of what he might answer.

It would help if he went back to the office, but he likes working from home because he can sit in his pants all day long, posting on the internet. His life is online. His job. His hobbies. He has identities online that I don't understand. Online, he says he's a non-binary wolf-human hybrid. He says he doesn't identify as fully human, but part wolf.

"Which part is wolf," I ask him, "because I'm not seeing it. Don't wolves go outside sometimes?"

"There's more than one way of understanding reality," he tells me. "I never knew you were such a bigot."

"Oh fuck off," I say.

But he doesn't fuck off. He comes to bed at four a.m. and puts his arms around me.

"Why do you put up with me," he asks.

"I don't know," I say. "Maybe I'm crazy too."

~

He's not the only one who doesn't believe there's a house on the moon. If he were the only one, I suppose it would make it easier. I could explain he was having a delusion. Get him to a doctor. But what if the doctor doesn't believe it either? I used to think most people were rational and sane but I've changed my mind.

Zoran used to be sane, I'm pretty sure. When I first met him, he liked running, and he used to carve little wooden birds from driftwood he found on the beach. I still have several of these birds, lined up on the windowsill in the bathroom, above the loose floorboard that Zoran was supposed to nail down. He says the birds trigger him now, but I still won't put them away. They remind me of when we got together. When he was my lovely Zoran. Back then, he would have laughed at the flat-earthers, the biology deniers, the no-housers. He's not the same person anymore.

"You've changed," I tell him.

"I've woken up," he says. "I wish you would too."

"How can you believe all this crap?"

"How can *you*?"

I go back to the observatory several times. It's always busy, there's always a queue. I usually recognise some of the people in it. And the prices keep going up. I'd buy my own telescope, except they are in high demand these days, and I can't really afford it. Plus I'm worried that Zoran would freak out if I forced him to look at the moon.

The house is still there, whenever I look for it.

I can see it with my own eyes.

So why does it seem less plausible now? Less real than it did before?

"You're getting inside my head," I tell Zoran.

"Good," he says. "You need to get past your prejudices. Educate yourself. And I don't mean with that stupid Brian Cox book."

"I like Brian Cox," I say.

"He's full of crap," says Zoran.

I go to my mum's for the weekend. It's like being a kid again, staying with my mum. I love it, but after a couple of days it drives me crazy. This time I don't want to go home, though.

"You can leave him," Mum says. "Not every relationship lasts forever."

"I love him, though," I say.

"Do you?" Mum asks. "Or do you love your memory of him? If you met him now, for the first time, would you get involved again?"

Eight years is a long time to throw away. Maybe I want kids, and it's getting too late to start over with someone else. But Zoran doesn't want kids anyway. He says we would be bringing them into a devastated hellscape. Maybe he's right.

"He's an idiot," Mum says. "What kind of a world would it be if people stopped having children?"

I don't know. I used to think Zoran would make a good dad. Before all this started. He used to love the outdoors. He knows how to camp, build fires, find edible mushrooms, hike across mountains. What kid wouldn't love all that?

"I'll take him away for the weekend," I say. "Into the woods or the mountains. He'll love that. It'll give him some perspective."

Mum nods, unconvinced. "Don't get your hopes up," she says.

I can't help it, though.

~

"Thank you," I say. "Thank you for doing this."

"No, it's good," says Zoran.

We're lying on our backs in the grass, gazing up at a sky that is freckled with stars. I reach for Zoran's hand and for once, he doesn't pull away from me.

"I still love you," I say, quietly. "I'm just scared."

"Scared of what?"

"Of you, a little bit? Of how you're changing."

Now he does pull his hand away. He sits up.

"I'm the one who should be scared," he says. "You're trying to control me. You're not letting me grow. You want me to be... I don't know what you want me to be."

I sit up too, and try to make eye contact with him, but he keeps turning his face away.

"I want you to be yourself! Just be yourself."

"So you're saying I'm not myself. If I'm not myself, what am I?"

"I don't know, Zoran." I sigh. "But I don't want to be in a fight with you."

"What you're not getting is that I *am* being myself. I'm more myself now than I've ever been.

When we were first together, I was trying to... live up to your idea of me. Impress you. I tried to be what you wanted. Now I'm being myself and you can't stand it. You can't just support me."

"I do support you," I say.

It's true. I've been paying his share of the rent and bills for weeks now, ever since he lost his job. How much more support should I give him? I can hear my mum's voice in my head, going, "bloody tell him that, then," but I can't. He seems so hurt.

"I'm sorry," I say into the silence. "I just worry. You're my boyfriend, I can't help worrying."

"And that's the other thing," he says. "You keep calling me your boyfriend. But you know I'm non-binary now."

"Okay!" I feel the blood rushing to my cheeks. "God, I'm sorry. I didn't think."

"I could have you fired from your job," he says.

Could he? But he wouldn't. Who'd pay his rent if I lost my job? "So what do you... how should I call you then?"

"You can say boyfriend. It's fine. But it's like, you should have asked me."

I think about this for a moment. "Sorry," I say. "I thought it was a joke."

"You think my identity's a joke?"

"No, I mean, I thought you were being ironic or something."

"This is awful," he says. "You're killing me."

He sleeps in the tent and says I shouldn't sleep in with him because my presence makes him feel traumatised. So I curl up in my coat, next to the fire, and in the morning, the birds are all singing and I wonder if they really are, or if any of this is really happening at all.

~

I meet a woman at the observatory. She's standing ahead of me in the queue and we get talking. When I've had my four minutes on the telescope, and come outside into the cold, she's waiting for me, huffing clouds of white air. It's freezing up there on the hill.

"Come for a drink," she says.

We're both wearing glasses that fog up when we walk into the bar, and we take them off and try to wipe them on our scarves. We're laughing, and I suddenly feel terrified by the lightness in my body, so I stop. I haven't laughed for a long time, I realise.

Iris is an artist. She shows me pictures on her phone. She's painting the interior of the house on the moon. I scroll through the images, wonderstruck. Her rooms are wild, full of colour and patterns, and incongruous things.

"Would you like to go there," she says, "if you could?"

"I would definitely go," I say. "My boyfriend would dump me, though."

"And that would be a bad thing?"

Iris has dark brown eyes that look bigger because the lenses in her glasses are so thick, and she has curly hair that springs out from under her woolly hat. She's beautiful, actually. I realise I'm staring at her, and that tears are rolling down my cheeks.

"I'm sorry," I say.

But Iris laughs. "You don't need to be sorry. You're just a human. Humans laugh and cry."

"I think my boyfriend has lost his mind," I say.

Iris nods. "You talk about him a lot," she says.

"I know," I say. I try to smile and I can feel it come out all wonky. "I've got nothing to say for myself anymore."

Walking home in the dark, hands shoved deep into my coat pockets, I feel as distant from my life as if I were in the house on the moon. In one of Iris's wild and vibrant rooms, with peacock wallpaper, and a giraffe reading a magazine in an armchair. I smile to myself. My life is absurd! But it doesn't have to be. I can leave him, I think. I can do it.

But when I walk into the flat and see him in the corner, slump-shouldered in front of his computer, the sadness comes over me again. Because I remember him before. When he was better. I feel like I'm failing.

"You went to the observatory," he says, not looking around.

"Yes," I say. "Then for a drink with Iris."

Now he swivels in his chair and looks at me. "Iris," he says.

"I'm allowed to have friends," I say.

He grunts, and turns back to the computer.

"Look, this isn't working," I tell him.

He ignores me.

"Zoran? I'm saying this is over. We're over."

"Okay," he says. "We're not, though."

I stand for a minute, staring at the back of his head. Turn around, I'm thinking, turn around and look at me. Listen to me.

He keeps click click clicking on the keyboard. Staring into the computer screen, where his real life is.

~

At four a.m. he comes to bed and wraps his arms around me.

"Don't do this," he says. "Don't do this to me."

"I'm not," I say. "I'm not doing anything."

"You can get help," he says. "You can be better."

I freeze. Hold my breath so I won't miss what he says next.

"You're just, like, wedded to these white supremacist notions of truth and objectivity," he says. "You have this rigid, binary view of the world. I hate to say it, but you're being a little fascist."

I wrench myself out from his embrace and run into the bathroom. The little wooden birds on the windowsill gaze up at me with their sightless eyes. You were real, I think, you were real! I swear it was all real. Zoran, with his laughing eyes, his clever hands, his way of making me feel like it was all going to be okay. I never thought it would be him who broke under the pressure of the last few years. I thought it would be him who held us together. Maybe that made it hard for him. Maybe I was part of the problem, expecting him to shoulder the burden for both of us. When everything shut down, when everyone was terrified, I thought he would be brave.

But instead of being brave, he broke.

I step back from the windowsill, onto the loose floorboard. My ankle turns and for a moment I think I'm going to fall but then I catch myself and I know I'm going to be okay.

~

Iris and I are walking in Inverleith park. The grass is white and icy, and the pond has thin sheets of frozen water for the swans to float on. I tell her about the birds.

"Maybe he's not the same person," she says.

"He's not," I say. "That's what I'm trying to tell you."

"No," she says. "I mean really not the same. What if the virus changed him? Or the vaccines?"

I sigh. I'm not sure what she's getting at. "I already told you everything," I say.

She grabs my arm so I stop walking, and gets right up close to my face.

"I'm saying he's actually *not* Zoran. Something happened. The real Zoran got taken. Destroyed by the virus."

"What?"

"It's obvious! You said it yourself. He's not the same. Ever since he got the virus, he's been a different person."

"Iris... "

"Just hear me out," she says. Her eyes look huge behind her glasses, with all her hair tied back under her hat. She looks so sincere, I want to laugh, or kiss her. I don't know.

But now she laughs at me. "Oh come on! I'm kidding!"

"Oh." I feel my face growing heated.

"I don't really think aliens stole your boyfriend," she says. She tucks her hand into my elbow and we start crunching over the frozen grass. "I do think he's a fucking loser, though. Just dump him, girl. Just end it."

~

When it's my turn for the telescope, I almost don't want to look through it. I know the house will be there. But what put it there? How is it there? I have so many questions now that I didn't have before. Am I being stupid and gullible, am I some kind of sheeple, like Zoran says? A little fascist, marching in lockstep? Is it really possible that they have doctored all the telescopes or drugged the water? They who? And then I put my eye to the lens and the moon resolves into its new shape, with its house like a hat, and I feel relief. And I feel resolve.

Walking home, I call Mum.

"You're doing the right thing," she says.

"You don't think I'm a fascist?"

Mum laughs. "No, you grew out of that when you turned six."

"I don't get why it's so hard," I say. "People break up all the time."

"Well it's simple," says Mum. "But that doesn't mean it's easy."

I let myself into the flat. Zoran is in his usual spot, facing the computer. His desk is littered with banana peels, empty noodle pots, coffee cups. I take my coat off, hang it up. He still hasn't looked at me.

"Zoran," I say.

His head lolls forward and I let out a little scream. Then he looks up at me and laughs.

"What's up?" he says.

"You scared me."

He rolls his eyes and turns back to the screen.

"I went to the observatory," I say.

"Uh huh."

"Zoran. I can't do this anymore. I'm breaking up with you. For real. And I mean it this time."

"No," he says.

"No? It's not a question."

"No," he says. "I'm breaking up with you."

He's still facing his screen. Breaking up with me while he stares into the computer, doing whatever it is he does.

"I can't take it anymore," he says. "You believe all this Daily Mail shit. You're violent..."

"Violent? How am I violent?"

"Your words are violent."

"Okay," I say. "Okay, whatever. Just leave, then. Please. You can go and stay with a friend tonight."

"What friend," he says. "What fucking friend? You've kept me away from my friends. I'm too embarrassed to have friends with you around."

He still hasn't looked at me. He's still clicking away.

"I'll go, then," I say. "I'll go and stay with Mum for a few days."

I'm shaking as I stuff clothes into a bag. I don't even know what I'm packing, it doesn't matter, take anything. I'll be okay, I tell myself. It'll be okay. I hear Zoran's chair scrape across the floor.

A roar comes from the bathroom.

"And you still keep these fucking birds even though you know they fucking trigger me you bitch!" He screams and then there is the sound of crashing glass and a heavy thud that shakes the whole flat.

I run to him.

He's lying across the bathroom floor, surrounded by shattered mirror shards and the tiny wooden birds that are scattered everywhere. For a moment I think he's in a pool of blood but it's just the bathmat under his head, and I kneel down beside him and say, "Zoran, baby, are you okay?"

He doesn't answer. His eyes are wide and staring at nothing. I push his shoulder and his head lolls away from me and I see a gash in the back of his skull. But there's no blood. There's nothing but a tangle of blue and red wires, a nest of cables where his brains should be.

~

They tell me I was screaming when they found us. They tell me I was covered in Zoran's blood. But I know it isn't true. I know what I saw.

Iris visits and brings me a framed picture of one of her moon rooms. It's the one I liked, of the giraffe reading a fashion magazine, and the peacock wallpaper.

"Do you want to come to the observatory," she says. "We could go together. It's been a while since you saw the house."

I shake my head. There's no house on the moon. I was wrong before. I was seeing what I was supposed to see.

That's what Zoran taught me. That there's more to the world than what's on the surface. That you have to see behind things, see through things. I should have trusted him.

Mum comes into my room and pulls the curtains open so that sunshine floods in.

"It's a beautiful day, love," she says. "A nice day for a walk. We could go and feed the ducks.

Listen to that lovely birdsong!" she says, pushing open the window.

"They're not birds," I say.

They're not real birds. If only I could make her see.

The Roses are Sighing

Where did you go, Wife? I looked for you all over the house. I looked in the wardrobes, the cupboards, the hide-and-seek places. I looked in the knife drawer, I rummaged through the cutlery. I opened matchboxes to see if you would spring out, your hair a cloud of wild, your spare teeth chattering behind your red lipstick.

The last thing I remember was the moon in our shadow. And you with your eye pressed to the lens of the telescope, watching as the moon and its little house were gradually covered in darkness. Our song was playing softly, from somewhere in the house. A moonlight serenade, when the moon went out.

~

Sooner or later they will find him. She opens the window and lets the light flood into the attic. It was the light he most particularly loved, their reason for coming here. You can believe in this light, he would say. You can believe anything you want in this light. She believes she will find him, perhaps sooner rather than later. Maybe even today.

She tells herself this, and she hugs herself in the chill of the day streaming in. Maybe it's even true. He had been standing right there, right beside her, staring into the telescope as the moon went out. She looked up into the sky as the moon began to flush with red, and when she looked back, he was gone.

She knows that men leave. But not this man. Not after so long. But what else can explain it? She's called all their old friends at the observatory, their former colleagues at the university, people she hasn't spoken to since she retired. No one answers the telephone.

Her bad shoulder aches from the cold, and she closes the window. Maybe she will find him, she thinks. Maybe it will be today.

~

Even after you retired, you watched the sky every night. We both did. When the house appeared, we both wished we were still working at the observatory. I remember those old days, when I would come into your room and you would say, "Can't you see that I'm working, Piggy?" You used to call me Piggy sometimes. When you were being a certain version of yourself. You put versions of yourself on and off like garments, and only I knew *you*: a little lost pea underneath that vast pile of coats. Sixty years, seventy. You get to know a person. Your hair went from cumulus to wispy cirrus. You forgot to put on your wig before you went out, but you never forgot your teeth. Your teeth, your natural teeth made of bone from your head: they were gone. Your new teeth were made of I don't know what. They began to have a yellowish tinge; you couldn't get to the orthodontist. Everything was closed that year. But you said you saw a light behind the glass. You hurt your shoulder trying to open the closed door.

You told me once that going through doors makes a person forget. There was a study done at some university or other. The doctor said it was dementia, but you said doors. Neither you or the doctor could prove anything, but from then on, the front door stayed closed, as final as a full stop. The winding sentences of the house ended there. You paced the ellipsis... the hallway... You put your coat on and put it off again. On and off. Off and on. You couldn't explain yourself, could you?

And I could not explain it either. Maybe we drifted apart.

~

The song that I sing is of moonlight... There is music coming from somewhere and it puts those words inside her head. The music drifts through the rooms of the house. It's the same music they were playing the night he stepped onto the moon, she recalls. As the engines powered down and he floated over the grey moon rocks, that song was playing through the open windows of the house. *Let us stray till break of day, in love's valley of dreams.* But was that true? It might only have been playing in her mind.

She definitely remembers him waltzing her around the kitchen, giddy with laughter, tripping over their feet. She remembers him standing breathless in the kitchen, telling her to come at once to the attic. He was panicking in case it was gone before she saw it. But it was there, the moon's little house. They made love on the floor, next to the telescope, in the light of the moon. "Soon," he said to her, and she agreed. "It's time," she said.

~

Sometimes words get trapped in my head and they buzz about in there like flies that can't find an open window. I don't know how to get them out. You were always very good with words, dear. Better than me.

Sometimes when I sit and think for a long time, I forget myself, and then I turn to you, forgetting that you have gone. I want to tell you things, to point at things and show you. They're going to send a rocket to the moon, to explore the house. It's a new space race, the newsreader says. I imagine some astronaut, bounding over the rocks, leaping towards the house and knocking the door. I imagine your laughter. Maybe they are playing our song inside the house on the moon. The astronaut will stand below a window, crooning. *"I stand at your gate and the song that I sing is of moonlight..."*

But I remember you when they first landed on the moon: leaning forward towards the television set, your eyes aglow like stars. Beautiful. I hope I told you that you were beautiful.

~

The garden is full of roses, but she doesn't go outside. She sits in the open windows and watches their silky dances in the wind. It's getting colder, and soon the roses will fade and die. Will he come back then? He liked to tend the roses. He pruned and fed them, and plucked them and presented them to her in bunches and bouquets, forgetting that their scent made her sneeze.

If only she could get into the garden, she could touch the roses, crush their velvet petals and score them with her nails. The roses are silver, like roses on the moon. But she cannot leave the house, in case he returns.

It is possible that he can only return if she leaves. The thought has occurred to her before. That they are like the wooden couple in a cuckoo clock they saw in Triberg, one figure sliding out on a roller, the other sliding in. They had spent an hour in the shop, pointing at the tiny things there, discussing whether they had room in their suitcases to bring something home. But this is not about clocks: she is a scientist at heart.

The roses are sighing... in love's valley of dreams. The song keeps coming back to her. Why? It was playing in the attic, the night they saw the moon go out. The last time she saw him.

The fragments of song repeat.

She is wondering if a song can bring him back.

~

You were always scheming, Wife. Always hiding, always thinking. I think if you were a ghost, you would haunt me. But you don't believe in ghosts, and neither do I. Except now I wonder. Because again the melody plays, from somewhere in the house that I cannot locate. It floods my dreams. *I wait for the touch of your hand in the June night.* I wait for the touch of your hand.

You never liked to wait. You were always so impatient. When the doctor gave us the bad news you leapt up from your seat while he was still talking. You said, "We can't waste time, Piggy. We can't waste any more time." But when we saw the house on the moon, you said, "I wish we had more time." And that night, the last night in the attic, you said, "It's time, my love."

He used to read to her from the horoscopes in the newspapers. "During a lunar eclipse, the Sun, Moon, and Earth line up in such a way that the Moon gets obscured by Earth's shadow. These lunations are known to stir the deep waters of our emotions. They magnetize dreams and memories to the surface and seek closure."

Are her memories being drawn up by the magnetic moon?

She remembers him reading the passage from the newspaper, and she remembers him saying, "Should it be then? Is that the right time?" It will never be the right time, there is no right time, she knows that now. The right time was the life they spent together, the time he spent brushing her hair, time measured in touches, in jokes, in songs. *My love, do you know that your eyes are like stars brightly beaming?* His eyes began to wonder, to grow strange and dim sometimes. There were moments before this that she lost him. They come back to her now.

They agreed no blood.

They piled cushions and duvets onto the attic floor. They played their favourite record, and said goodbye to the moon.

She wonders if the song will let them go.

~

So don't let me wait, come to me tenderly in
the June night
I stand at your gate and I sing you a song in
the moonlight
A love song, my darling, a Moonlight
Serenade

Here Come Old Flat-Top

Infinity means never ending. Outwards and ever outwards. First your hands and the shape of your body, then your bed with the princess bedspread and the magnolia-on-woodchip walls and the ceiling with the polystyrene tiles. Up through the space in the attic where something moulders and scratches, and through the roof and over the roof, above the house. The grey blur of clouds and the moon and the few peeping stars you can see in the sky. Past those, into the deeper space beyond. The solar system and the Milky Way. Past the stars to more stars and more stars and more blackness peppered with silver, more blackness expanding into blackness. The same blackness under your eyelids in the dark bedroom.

Focus on the pink colour of the bedspread, the wide eyes of the princess, her crown. Pick up your book and look at the words one by one without reading. The universe keeps expanding and you cannot make it stop. It keeps going away from you until you are so small, you are nothing. You are an invisible speck of nothing on a planet that is an invisible speck of nothing, revolving around a sun that is nothing but a tiny grain of heat and light that will one day go out.

But remember the moon. Remember the moon with its little house. One day you can go there. One day you *will* go there, and then you'll understand.

~

Think about a yellow car with the doors left open, a yellow car slung sideways across the road. The faces of strangers peering down, reassuring hands on your hands. The looping whirl of a siren.

She just walked out, she didn't look where she was going. A white woman in a navy suit stands over you, twisting her hands together over and over. *I didn't see her, she walked right in front of the car. I couldn't stop.* There are other people, her family perhaps, holding onto the woman's arms, weighing her down like ballast.

Where are your family? Why are you lying alone in the road, with the yolk flooding out of your cracked egg head?

There are white coats so luminous that they burn your eyes, and there is your mother's face, her gap-toothed mouth, her dry kisses, no tears. Nobody cries. You must not cry.

Your head is sewn and bandaged. Blood stains on your princess bedspread. No one is at home in the daytimes, only you. Your mind keeps coming loose from your body. It's always drifting up into the universe and dissolving into space.

~

I knock on the door. The first time. You understand: I have to be invited in. You come to the door in your too-small pyjamas, with your head still caked in a rusty bandage, your wide eyes hollowed out with exhaustion.

You don't know when Mummy will be home? I'll come in and wait, then. You stand aside, biting your nails, not knowing the right thing to do. You want to be good, don't you? You want to be a good little girl.

You are a good girl. You take your gifts carefully, gratefully. They are princess things, things stolen from fairytales. A crown, for your little broken head. Dresses and a sparkling wand, and crystal slippers. And now for my gifts. White Lightning. Golden Virginia. You twirl and twirl in your princess dress. When you fall down, throw up, lie back dizzy, you're alone again.

~

Your mother screams through the open doors of your house. How could you do this to her? You don't care about her. She'll kill herself if that's what you want. Is that what you want?

What have you done? you wonder. Tiptoeing carefully around her, slinking back against the walls, the seam of your sewn-up head glowing with pain.

Your mother pulls the sheets off your bed. She's sobbing. Look what you've done to her. She can't cope.

She can't cope.

You want to cry but that will make everything worse. So instead, you hide in the bottom of the wardrobe, in the dark nest of discarded things. Picture the universe, rushing away from you. Outward and ever outward. But now your attention snags on the moon. Wouldn't you like to live in the house on the moon? The house is a castle and you're the princess. You have your crown, brittle with stars and dry blood. You're the ruler and no one can tell you what to do.

~

You're woken by the sounds of music and laughter, the acrid smell of cigarettes, the jangling quality of voices talking over one another. It's nonsense time again.

Creep out of the wardrobe, and sit at the top of the stairs. From here, you can watch the people writhing. Your mother blowing out gusts of smoke towards the ceiling, a man cupping her breast in his hand. The record changes and they play my song, the beat sneaking up and catching you unawares. You tap your feet.

here come old flat-top he come grooving up slowly he got juju eyeballs he one holy roller

Who put this crap on, they say. A man staggers out of the living room, sees you sitting at the top of the stairs. Hey, he says, hey you. You dart back inside your room, back into the wardrobe, back to your house on the moon. Wouldn't you like to stay there, always?

he say one and one and one is three got to be good looking cause he's so hard to see

There won't be any nonsense-time on the moon. No creaking steps of someone in your room. No heavy breath panting at the wardrobe door. Your mother's voice calling up the stairs. Frank, she yells. Is that his name? There won't be a Frank on the moon. Say his name in your mind over and over. It's a silly name. A nonsense name. It's never nonsense time on the moon.

~

That crack in your head, that's how I got in. The next time I come I don't need to knock. Your gifts are moon cakes, pale pink with green insides. They taste so sweet they make you feel dizzy. They make your head pound. The bandage feels too tight, like your head is trying to expand. You put on your crown and at once you feel better. You were born to be a princess, not a slave. In the house on the moon you can have all the slaves you like.

Come here and sit on my knee. You don't like that? My grizzled beard, my nicotine stains? You think you are any better, in your ragged pyjamas, your dirty bandaged head? You bite your nails to the quick. It looks ugly. Why doesn't your mother tell you not to do that? You know why not, don't you? You can call me Old Flat-top. It's one of my names. I'm not your father, but if you hung me upside-down I would be.

got to be a joker he just do what he please

Ask me about the house on the moon. What it's like there, how you would live. Close your eyes and you can be there now. A pink and gold marble staircase winds around the inside of the house. The floors are shiny and you can slide on them in your socked feet and there are a thousand rooms and in every room is something quite wonderful: moon cakes and trifles and platters full of chicken nuggets and rooms full of dresses with big skirts you can twirl in and rooms full of rocking horses and dolls houses and lego. And everything makes sense there. It's never nonsense-time.

You don't want to come back, I know.

There's a spell that can take you there forever. Should I tell you what it is?

~

Your mother won't get out of bed today. She lies with her face to the wall and when you come close she snarls and orders you away. You, stupid girl that you are, ask her if she loves you. You're checking, aren't you? You think Old Flat-top is telling you porky pies? Your mother says she loves cigarettes. Make me a cigarette, she says.

you one holy roller

You lick the paper and stick it down.

Light it for me, she says.

Your head hurts where it broke in two. It's a pain like an ache and a slap all rolled together. When you inhale the cigarette smoke you feel poison seeping along the stitched seam of your scalp. You choke. Your mother laughs. Give that to me. You're too young. Your mouth tastes acrid and vile, head spinning with nausea.

She drops the cigarette in the bedclothes and you fish it out for her. Pat the bedclothes down to put out the sparks. She's going to burn the house down one of these days.

~

It's nonsense time again.

You tell Frank you're going to tell your mummy. But Frank laughs and says she already knows and if you don't shut up you're going to wake her and then it's going to be worse.

You leave your body and go travelling in space. Up to the moon, to your castle with its moat of stars. I'm there, waiting for you. My princess. Silk carpets under your feet.

Think about moon cakes. Think about cakes towered high with layers of buttercream frosting. Vats of hot chocolate with whipped cream and marshmallows. You could be having a princess feast right now. If you look out of the window, you'll see the Earth, thousands of miles away. So far away that it cannot touch you, that nothing on the Earth can harm you.

~

Take your time. Sit on your bed and think it over. Infinity is never ending. Outwards and ever outwards. First your hands and the shape of your body, then your bed with the stained and ruined princess bedspread and the magnolia-on-woodchip walls where your handprints have dirtied the paint and the ceiling with the broken polystyrene tiles. Up through the space in the attic where something moulders and scratches, and through the roof and over the roof, above the house. And up to the—

Focus on the pink colour of the bedspread, the wide eyes of the princess, her crown. Pick up your book and look at the words one by one without reading. Listen to Frank snoring, next to your mother. They'll sleep through the end of the world.

The universe keeps expanding but you can make it stop. You don't have to be nothing, an invisible speck of nothing. You can be something. Everything. You can be a princess. Think about the moon with its little house. Think about the rooms full of books and dresses and no one touching you. No one finding your hiding places. There's only you.

Only you and me.

I'm here now. I'm standing beside you. I'm putting the matches into your dirty little hands.

come together right now

In Maksimir Park

We're walking in autumnal blaze. The leaves are russet and gold, falling. Sycamore seeds helicopter from the trees and spiral around us. The lakes are pale blue in the centre and dark at the edges, like eyes. No one is there, except for the two of us.

We walk down an aisle between trees that reach up like a cathedral. Her gloved hand in mine. Our boots scuff the patchwork of fall colours. We wade through knee-high drifts of leaves. Are we laughing? I think we laugh.

And she says, "Don't go."

But she says it under her breath, and so softly that I can pretend she hasn't said it at all.

~

She catches a whirling sycamore seed and holds it up to me like a prize win at the fairground. "Look," she says. She pushes the seed deep inside my coat pocket. "It won't grow there, baby," I say. "Something might grow," she replies.

I lean towards her, to kiss her, but the ground gives way beneath me. She catches my arm as I fall, but she can't hold me. Painful blotches melt inside my eyelids. I try to breathe. Try to remember my training. I'm ready for this. I'm ready. Maya's voice echoes around me and erupts into a soul-shattering sound. A terrible shaking breaks out beneath my body, becomes my body, shakes my organs, my blood, my brain against my skull, my bones against my flesh. A roar like the end of the world vibrates through my marrow, makes me feel like I'm a drum, being struck by God's hands.

"What's happening? Are you okay?"

Maya's sitting on the ground with me, on the path, in the leaves.

"Nothing," I say. "I'm fine. Get up. You'll dirty your coat."

I stand and help her to her feet, even though I feel wobbly myself. I pull her into my arms.

"I love you," I say. "I remember all of this."

~

We make for a bench at the edge of the path, looking out across a green field bordered by high trees wearing vibrant clothes of ruby and gold. In the middle of the field, an old oak tree twists around itself, reaching wizened black hands towards the sky. Maya takes off her scarf and lays it on the bench for us to sit upon. She says that's why Americans are fat and sick, because they don't take proper precautions like this.

"I'm not fat or sick," I say.

"Because I take precautions for you." She smiles.

"Well, lucky me." I put an arm round her, kiss her forehead through her woolly hat. She smells like expensive perfume, clean cashmere, soap, face powder, wet leaves, rocket fuel. "Let's go back to the hotel," I say. "We've got the whole day."

"Not yet," says Maya. She squeezes my hand and we sit in silence for a while, watching the leaves drifting across the path. A black squirrel darts up the oak tree, glancing round comically at us to see if we're going to cause him a problem. Crows gather around the tree, black and grey like they're in morning suits. They call to one another, and I wonder what they're saying, what information they're passing on.

Maya says, "We need to talk."

"Okay?"

"Don't go," she says.

This time she says it loud enough that I can't pretend I haven't heard. The roar of her voice becomes a physical force, sinking through me. My skin drags back from my face, my eyeballs are pulled back in my head and I know this is too much, this weight is going to crush me. This is madness, trying to push through this forcefield, trying to puncture the black mysteries of the universe.

Madness. Hubris. That's Maya's word. Maya, Maya, Maya. I repeat her name in my mind, hardly able to hear it over the roaring engine. Unable to picture her face because my eyes are shaking, my body is being crushed, my soul is being compressed and tortured until it feels atomic.

~

We scramble up a path through trees, coming out on a scraped little field and a church. It's half fallen down, held up by scaffolding and draped in long nets. "The earthquakes," Maya says. "They seemed to strike the churches more than anything else."

"I hadn't noticed that," I say. "All of Zagreb seems to have cracked." I say, "Let's go inside." She shakes her head, but I grab her hand and she lets me pull her along, under the scaffold and into the chill damp church.

There's birds nesting in the altar. Puddles on the stones. Maya makes the sign of the cross; she can't help herself. I don't say anything. I gave up on all that a long time ago. Maya tells me they've been praying on things at her church. Praying on the house. On the mission. On me. I say, "That's alright. But prayers aren't going to make a difference."

I kiss her. "I love you," I say. I hold her face between my hands. "It's going to be okay."

"You don't seem okay," she says. "Something's wrong."

"No," I say. "Everything's fine."

"Don't you think they should have stopped things, after what happened to Mike?"

I sigh. "Mike was crazy, baby. He lost his mind."

"He went through the same tests, the same training as you did. People like you don't go crazy."

"Anyone can go crazy."

"Not Mike."

I don't want to talk about this. I smile and walk away from her, towards the stone window in the still-standing side of the church.

A pencil floats past my head, followed by a chocolate bar.

Maya is humming a tune. It takes me a moment, but I recognise it's that song, the one they're going to play when we land on the moon. It's catchy, but I wish it was something with more gravitas. I'm not sure we really need a theme tune anyway. Isn't it enough that we're going?

"I'm pretty sure she wrote it just to torture us," I say.

"No," says Maya. "She wrote it for Mike."

I frown. "She didn't even know Mike."

"They met at her party. The night it happened. She wrote about it." Maya closes her eyes for a moment, as if summoning the memory. "*A fist through the heart and one through the throat. When they told me you were gone that's how I felt. And I remembered when you were in my hands, now you're standing on the dream of the pioneer's land.*"

"Something's wrong."

The moon fills the window, bulges its belly towards us, tips its hat. The blue-green Earth has dwindled away but it doesn't feel like I'm expanding, but like that crazy beautiful marble is lodged somewhere in my chest. Like a bullet slowly working its way to my heart.

~

A siren is wailing, looping shrill wails that reverberate through my mouth and eyes. I'm lashed to my ship, strapped in to my flight chair. Struggling to undo the ties and get out.

Pam Aishwarya is slamming her hands against the console, over and over, hitting screens that blare light and sound then fade to black. She turns and sees me.

"Something's wrong," says Pam Aishwarya.

I sink back into my seat.

Pam hunches over her console, her flight suit making her look bulky and stegosaurus-like in silhouette. Control console lights up over my head. It all looks alien, incomprehensible. Lights and symbols like hieroglyphs in an ancient tomb. I don't know what anything means. Red globules float over my head, obscuring my view of the console.

"Something's wrong," I say.

Pam Aishwarya nods in my direction. "You noticed, huh." Her voice is curt, unfriendly.

I finally manage to unstrap myself from my flight seat.

"What happened? I passed out? Did the explorer launch? Where are we?"

I drift over to Pam's side. On the monitor I see the little explorer vehicle bouncing over rocks.

"Orbit. Dark side," says Pam. "I don't know what happened. We all passed out, I guess."

"All of us? Where's Troy?"

Something red floats in front of me, a large, shining, wobbling disk.

"What the fuck is that?" I ask.

Pam doesn't even acknowledge the questions. I rotate myself to look around the capsule. Troy's strapped into his flight chair, blood snaking up out of his flight suit. I move towards him, breaking the red globules that bulge and float like in a lava lamp. I touch my gloved fingers to his neck, not feeling anything through my gloves. But I don't need to feel anything. I can see from the pallor of his skin, his opened, rolled-back eyes. The hundreds of slashes and tears in his flight suit where his blood escapes and floats free.

"What happened?" I'm whispering. Trying to keep the fear from my voice.

Pam's watching me now, her expression serious and withholding.

"I don't know," she says, carefully measuring out her words. "Maybe he did it to himself."

"Like Mike did?" I say.

"I don't know," she says again. "The last thing I remember is coming into orbit, seeing the house from the porthole. We were all crowded around. We must have launched the explorer, because it's down there."

I try to think: what do I remember?

On the monitor, the explorer bounces and rolls along, over rocks and rugged gravel. The house is in view now from the explorer's camera. It looks immense, the way the pyramids look immense when you approach them on foot. It's like some great Neolithic mega-structure. A tribute to some alien god.

I look at Pam. We're staring at one another, as if we think the answers are somewhere inside the other's brain.

"I don't remember anything after we launched," I say.

"It's because we're on the dark side," says Pam. "It's not affecting us now. We're not under its influence."

I look back at the monitor. Then at Troy, or what's left of him, anyway. He was my friend. We trained together. But I don't feel anything, except for dread and fear that races cold through my bones.

~

"Forty-two minutes," says Pam Aishwarya.

I'm trying to catch Troy's blood in bags, to clear the space. I've covered Troy's body with foil blankets. After a while, I realise there's silence in my snoopy cap.

"Ground control?" I say.

Pam shakes her head. "We're cut off on this side. We'll be back on line in... forty minutes."

"But in forty minutes, we might be... I don't know."

Pam Aishwarya sighs angrily. "Any suggestions, hotshot? Or am I just waiting around for you to go crazy and kill me too?"

"I didn't kill Troy," I say. "I don't know what happened, but I know that couldn't have been me."

Pam nods, accepting this. But if I didn't kill Troy, I think, that leaves Pam. There's no way he could have done that to himself. Was Pam capable of that? What did she mean, under the influence of the moon?

Pam says, "I was at home, with my family. The kids playing in the backyard. I could feel the sun on my face and my arms. I really felt it. It wasn't like a dream, but I suppose it must have been."

"I was with Maya," I say. "It wasn't a dream."

"Then this must be the dream," says Pam.

I look around the capsule, taking in the cold metal, plastic, the glassy consoles, the bulkheads, Troy's body bundled into foil blankets.

"Abort mission," I say.

"I don't think we can do that. I don't know how. And by the time we get back in contact with Ground Control, it'll be too late."

It's like she's punched me in the chest. In that moment, I think maybe I could kill Pam

Aishwarya. I could tear her limb from limb. But the fury passes through me quickly, replaced by a sickening dread.

"Abort dream," I say.

"Thirty-six minutes," says Pam.

~

It's illegal to dispose of a dead body in space. I remember that from my training. It was a joke then, a light hearted factoid to leaven the burden of heavy learning. Now I'm wondering if they knew back then. If they were trying to warn us.

Troy's body is a strange disturbance.

We need to turn the craft around, somehow. Get out of the moon's orbit. Abandon the explorer. Go home. But none of that is possible without comms. And we won't have comms until we swing back around to the light side of the moon. Back under the influence of the house.

Pam's turned the explorer's monitor off. She says we're not supposed to know, not supposed to explore something like this. Something sacred.

"That's crazy," I say. "We're scientists. Explorers. Pioneers."

"Don't say that," says Pam. "It reminds me of that stupid song."

I stare at her, memories coalescing in my mind.

"It's about Mike," I say. "The song. Maya explained it all. She never understood how they

- 118 -

found his hand outside the lab when his body was inside."

"If Mike had lived, you wouldn't be on this mission," said Pam.

"Shit."

We both slump back, or we would, if there was enough gravity for slumping.

"It's hopeless, isn't it?" I say.

"Twenty-two minutes," says Pam.

We prepare an emergency message to be broadcast to ground control as soon as we're in range. We're sending it over and over again. Troy's dead. One of us might be next. Abort mission.

We record messages to our loved ones, too.

Maya, I say. *I love you. I will always remember that day in Maksimir Park. I don't think even death can take that away.*

"Twelve minutes," says Pam.

We debate the permutations of one of us tying the other to the flight seat. Pam thinks I should be the one tied down. I'm most likely to be the killer, in her opinion. Men kill more than women, that's true. But aren't women more ruled by the moon? The old Pam would have scoffed at that, but now she simply gives a grim nod. The truth is we have no idea which of us killed Troy. We decide to strap ourselves into our flight seats, and do our best to secure ourselves with knots and bindings.

We secure ourselves with three minutes to go. Already I can see the glimmer of light at the edge of the porthole. A glowing penumbra, an eye opening and swallowing us up.

You were right, Maya. I should have listened when you told me not to go. I should have listened.

~

The rain has hardened and intensified while we've been inside the derelict church. It drips through the holes in the roof, patters on the puddled flagstones.

Somehow we've moved so we're standing at opposite ends of what remains of the aisle. She's standing by the altar and I'm nearer the doors, in a weird inversion of our wedding day. I remember watching her walk to me in her white dress with a veil over her face. She was wearing high heels that made her as tall as her father, and under her veil I could see dark eyes and red lipstick. I didn't know what I was feeling in that moment. The room was swollen with music, with emotion.

Now her red lipstick and dark eyes glow in the gloom of the church, and I realise that I feel afraid.

I walk towards her down the rubble-strewn aisle. An icy droplet of rain splashes my forehead. Maya laughs, but it's a hard, harsh sound echoing in the space.

"Here comes the bride," she says.

"Let's go home. It's raining."

"Americans," she says. "You can send a rocket to the moon, but a bit of rain's too much for you."

I'm standing in front of her now. Her eyes are hard, so hard that I barely recognise her face. I reach out and encircle her wrist with my hand. Her fragile bones.

"Don't do it," says Maya, a warning tone in her voice.

What does she mean? What does she think I'm going to do? I drop her wrist and she holds it to her chest, cradling it and looking at me reproachfully, like it's a puppy I've kicked. I didn't hurt her. I know that. I would never.

"Let's get out of this place," I say. "It's giving me the creeps."

"You know what really happened to Mike, don't you?" Maya says. "And Troy? You know what happened to Troy."

"Shut up," I say. "Shut up, shut up, shut up."

She laughs, and stands aside so that I can see the altar. The body is laid over the stone, wrapped in foil blankets, steaming lightly in the cold rain.

"Sacrifices," says Maya. "Sacrifices to the moon."

"That makes no sense," I say.

"Don't go," says Maya. "I'm warning you."

I pull the foil away from Troy's body. As I peel the blankets away from him, red globules of his blood lift away from his flight suit and wobble into the air. They drift up towards the roof, pierced by rain, snagging on the birds nests and broken tiles.

"It's my dream," I say.

But Maya is silent. She is no longer standing beside me.

The church is empty.

~

I run out of the church, onto the path, into the woods. I'm calling her name but it echoes in silence. Blood rains upwards through the trees. So much blood.

It's on my hands, on Pam's hands. On our faces.

My pockets are full of sycamore seeds. Something might grow, Maya once said. But nothing grows in space.

The moon laughs and drinks our blood.

Sycamore seeds fall in the spaceship and blood rises in the forest. We orbit around this tiny, terrible dream forever, unable to tear ourselves away from its beauty.

Also by Georgina Bruce:

Novellas
Honeybones (TTA Press, 2020)

Collections
This House of Wounds (Undertow Publications, 2019)

Now available and forthcoming from Black Shuck Shadows:

Now available and forthcoming from Black Shuck Shadows:

Now available and forthcoming from Black Shuck Shadows:

blackshuckbooks.co.uk/shadows

6/6/24